All in with an Outlaw . . .

The air filled with billows of white gun smoke, and dust kicked up as Slocum thrust about, fighting to get to his feet. Stringfellow backed away, still firing. His six-gun came up empty at the same instant Slocum's did.

The exchange had alerted the outlaws inside the cabin, but Slocum knew escape lay in capturing Stringfellow, not in running. He dived forward as the gang leader slipped around the corner of the building. His fingers closed on the man's leg. He hung on for dear life and was dragged along a couple feet before Stringfellow lost his balance and crashed flat on his back. He tried kicking Slocum in the belly, but desperation gave Slocum strength.

He caught the foot and twisted savagely, rolling Stringfellow over. Slocum dropped down, the foot still captive in his armpit. He felt muscles in the outlaw's leg protest and tear. Then strong hands pulled him away.

He hadn't expected the men inside to come boiling out this fast. Slocum kicked and twisted and even got his Colt yanked free, only to remember that it was empty when pulling the trigger resulted in a dull click.

"Hold that son of a bitch," Stringfellow growled. He kicked away, tried to stand, and fell when his injured leg betrayed him. "He busted my damned leg!"

JAKE LOGAN

SLOCUM
AND THE
PACK OF LIES

J

JOVE BOOKS, NEW YORK

THE BERKLEY PUBLISHING GROUP
Published by the Penguin Group
Penguin Group (USA) LLC
375 Hudson Street, New York, New York 10014

USA • Canada • UK • Ireland • Australia • New Zealand • India • South Africa • China

penguin.com

A Penguin Random House Company

SLOCUM AND THE PACK OF LIES

A Jove Book / published by arrangement with the author

For information, address: The Berkley Publishing Group,
a division of Penguin Group (USA) LLC,
375 Hudson Street, New York, New York 10014.

ISBN: 978-0-515-15490-0

PUBLISHING HISTORY
Jove mass-market edition / September 2014

PRINTED IN THE UNITED STATES OF AMERICA

10 9 8 7 6 5 4 3 2 1

Cover illustration by Sergio Giovine.

1

Sweat broke out on John Slocum's forehead, and it wasn't only because of the heat boiling from the potbellied stove a couple feet behind him. The saloon door was closed tight against the growing chill of a late Idaho autumn. Tobacco smoke billowed in thick clouds, choking some of the wranglers circling the table and watching the poker game.

Slocum dropped his cards facedown on the table. There wasn't any need to look at them again. Two pairs. Kings over eights with a solitary ace to keep them company. Not great, but he had to play the hand. Every cent he had earned over a season of working as a drover lay on the table. The tinhorn gambler across from him might have a better hand, but Slocum doubted it unless he tried cheating. With every move he made obvious to the entire crowd, the gambler had a hard time palming a card. The deal was done. Only playing—bluffing—was left.

Slocum couldn't fold, and the gambler knew it. If he did, he had no chance at winning back his wages. But the gambler had a few dollars left to raise. If Slocum couldn't call, the pot was lost.

"Well, now, partner," the gambler drawled, "I think you don't have squat in that hand of yours. Now me, well, I got a straight flush. No way am I gonna fold with that."

Slocum remained alert, watching the man's long-fingered, almost effeminate hands as they restlessly moved the cards in his hand in an endless shuffle. A card hidden up a lace-trimmed cuff might be swapped for one of the pasteboards. Or a card slid back and dropped into the man's lap so he could bend and pick up another, better card. Slocum's eagle-eyed stare prevented any of that from happening. If he let the gambler cheat him now, it would be a long, hungry winter.

He didn't even want to consider that the gambler actually had a better hand. Whatever the tinhorn had, it wasn't a straight flush, but it might be three of a kind. Or even a straight. Too many hands beat Slocum. But not this time. He read men well and the gambler wasn't sure what he had.

"I got three dollars left. I raise you the whole lot of these here greenbacks." The gambler shoved forward the last of his money.

Slocum kept his eyes on the gambler's hands as he reached into his vest pocket and drew out his watch.

"This is worth more than three dollars. I call."

"Wait, let me look." The gambler reached across the table, his body momentarily hiding his hand. Slocum moved like a striking snake and shoved the gambler back into his chair so hard he skidded a foot away from the table.

"One of you," Slocum said, addressing the crowd, "pass the watch over to him so he can see it's worth at least twenty dollars."

One of the eager onlookers did as requested. Slocum kept from smiling. The panicky look that flashed across the gambler's face told the story. He was bluffing and had intended to improve his cards by sleight of hand.

"Mighty fine-lookin' watch, mister," the cowboy said, and he let it spin a couple times before holding it out for the gambler.

"It'll do."

Slocum waited for the watch to go back to the pot. That watch was his brother's legacy. Robert had been killed at the Angles during Pickett's Charge. A downed soldier's belongings were shared. Slocum was lucky the watch had made its way back, going from one veteran's hand to another, to Slocum's Stand in Calhoun, Georgia, where he could claim it. He had killed more than one man who thought to steal it, but now Slocum worried at the hint of desperation in his own behavior. If the gambler won, it would because Slocum had chosen to make the watch part of the bet.

"Let's see your cards." Slocum turned over his hand, his eyes never leaving the gambler's face. The flicker of fear that passed across it was quickly replaced with one of avarice.

Slocum moved again like a striking snake, half coming out of his chair to slam his hand down hard on the gambler's wrist. With his hand pinned to the table, the man couldn't move. Slocum felt his muscles twitching in strain.

"One of you boys, take his cards and show them to everybody."

"I'll do it," piped up the man who had examined the watch. He pulled the cards from the gambler's grip. "Lookee there. Two pair."

Slocum looked down and saw the gambler's cards. Jacks and tens.

The gambler had lost.

Slocum released the captive wrist and saw a third jack flutter from the sleeve to the sawdust-covered floor. He said nothing about it as he raked in the pot. The first thing he did was tuck away his watch and then start sorting out the greenbacks and coins on the table.

With the suddenness of a lightning flash, the table went flying as a man crashed against it. Slocum grabbed a handful of bills. The rest of the pot scattered across the saloon floor, sending the crowd who had passively watched into action rooting through the sawdust like pigs at a trough.

The gambler laughed. A sneer crossed his lips. He silently told Slocum he had lost—they both had. The saloon's customers were the only winners in this game.

Slocum stared down at the man struggling to keep his balance against the table. Then he looked through a gap in the crowd and saw a man all squared off and ready to throw down. He had a scar across his eyebrow that left a pink canyon amid a dark black brow and weathered forehead. A long, hooked nose curled above a bushy mustache, and lips pulled back like a feral wolf spotting dinner.

"Ain't nobody says that to me and lives," the man growled. His voice had a rasp to it like a rusted file dragging across iron. His right hand twitched above the butt of a Colt .44.

Slocum had seen men like this before. They took offense because it gave them a reason to kill. They would be just as happy wildly flinging lead in all directions to take a half-dozen lives, but they were cunning enough to realize that got them invited to a necktie party by the survivors. Singling out one man and killing him gave enough wiggle room so only family and devoted partners argued over the death.

"You just cost me a hundred dollars," Slocum said. He tucked away what money he had rescued from the table. The scrambling across the saloon floor continued unabated, telling him some of the pot—his pot—had yet to be harvested.

"You butt out. This is 'tween me and that lily-livered, mangy liar. Nobody calls me what he did."

"Honest, I wasn't talkin' to you. It was my—"

The gunman moved with a quick, smooth motion to draw his six-shooter. Slocum noted how comfortable the man was, how he reached across and fanned off a couple rounds. Given other circumstances, both rounds would have buried themselves in the victim's gut. A man on hands and knees hunting for Slocum's winnings bumped into the shooter's leg and caused the second round to go astray.

Slocum let out a yelp of pain as the slug tore through his hat brim and creased his skull. His head snapped back, and he fell hard to the floor. The room spun about him until he blinked his eyes and cleared his vision. With a head screaming from the painful wound, he pushed his way to his feet and wobbled just a little. This saved his life. The gunman fanned off another round in his direction. The slug dug another chunk from Slocum's hat brim and exploded against the mirror behind the bar. This got the barkeep's attention.

"You're payin' fer that, mister!"

Slocum braced himself against the bar. His hand went to the Colt Navy in his cross-draw holster and brought it around. His thumb caught the hammer and drew it back. His finger tightened on the trigger. A .36-caliber round blasted past one customer and hit the gunman in the left thigh. The man yelped and grabbed for the wound, but experience took over. He began firing as fast as he could in Slocum's direction. The drunk rooting about on the floor for the dropped money chose that instant to rear up. This saved Slocum. The gunman's bullet caught him in the back of the head.

Blood and brains sprayed against Slocum's duster.

By now the crowd screamed and rushed about, dropped money forgotten. The cowboys tried to get behind overturned tables or flee through the front door. One fell through a window amid crashing glass. This brought the barkeep around, screaming. When he unlimbered a sawed-off shotgun, anyone with good sense dived for the floor. Slocum hit an instant before buckshot ripped through the spot where he had stood at the bar. He grunted as men tumbled atop him. He shoved them off and brought his six-gun up to get another shot at the gunman who had started the fracas.

All Slocum saw was the man's back as he retreated through the window that had just been busted out. Grunting, Slocum shoved his way back to his feet, only to find himself staring down the double barrels of the bartender's scattergun.

"Better lower that," Slocum said in a low voice. He had faced death so many times he knew when to be scared. The barkeep was frightened and angry but not to the point he would do anything foolish like cut down a man who wasn't threatening him.

"You—you started all this! You're gonna pay for it!"

Slocum used the barrel of his Colt to move the shotgun away from dead center on his chest. The curiously gentle move did more to calm the bartender than if Slocum had spoken.

"You started it!"

"The man who gunned him down's responsible." Slocum tilted his head in the direction of the man who had crashed into the poker table. He lay sprawled on his back, deader than a doornail. "Who is he? A regular customer?"

"Petey Hammersmith," the barkeep said, standing on tiptoe to peer over the bar. As he stretched, he laid the shotgun down. Slocum shoved it away out of reach. "Damnation, who's gonna tell his old lady he upped and got himself shot? They ain't been married a year. She might need a powerful lot of consolin'."

"The other fella started it," said the man who had examined the pocket watch and had been first to dive for spilled money. He clutched a few silver dollars in his grimy fist. "I think that was the outlaw the marshal's been huntin' fer."

"Somebody had better get the marshal," Slocum said. He stepped away from the bar, winced as he peeled his hat brim away from his forehead. Blood oozing from the crease had already begun to dry but not enough to keep it from threatening Slocum's vision if it trickled down past his eyebrow. A nearby bar rag sopped up the sluggish flow of blood from his head wound. Another inch lower and he would have been buried alongside Petey Hammersmith.

"That outlaw fellow, he started it. Petey didn't do nuthin'. He jist came in for a drink, nuthin' more."

Slocum let the barkeep and the witnesses get their story straight. From what he had seen, the dead man had been the victim. He hadn't worn a side arm, though he carried a hunting knife in a sheath at his right hip. Slocum stepped over a couple men who had returned to scrounging for dropped money and stood in the doorway.

That almost cost him his life.

Three shots tore into the door frame and showered him with splinters. He bent low and dived, skidding along the rough-hewn boardwalk until he found shelter behind a stack of crates. Pushing against them warned him he might be out of sight but wasn't out of danger. The crates were empty. To prove what trouble he was in, another slug ripped through the box at his right and dug its way into the saloon wall.

Chancing a quick look around the edge gave Slocum a view of the outlaw across the street, resting his hand against a hitching rail to get better aim. Without aiming, Slocum fired a couple rounds in the man's direction not only to disturb his aim but to convince him to hightail it.

Two more shots came in Slocum's direction before the outlaw lit out. Slocum rose and aimed, firing once more. He missed. The next trip of the hammer smashing down produced a dull click. He was out of ammo. Cursing, he took time to reload. When he again carried a full cylinder, he hunted for any sign that the town marshal had arrived. All he saw was a man coming from an abandoned store to look around curiously.

The scene fixed in Slocum's brain as if it had been etched on metal.

"Get down!" His warning fell on deaf ears.

The outlaw fired and the inquisitive bystander sank to his knees, holding his side. Slocum ran into the street, firing as he went. He tried to aim but running and firing at the same time sent his lead flying about wildly. Skidding to a halt beside the wounded man gave him the chance to aim better. His final two rounds sent the outlaw scurrying away.

"You hit bad?"

"Been shot before," the man grated out, "but nuthin' like this. I feel all wet inside, like my innards are sloshin' about."

He looked down to where blood oozed between his fingers. "Is this as bad as it looks?"

"I'll get you to the doctor." Slocum reloaded as he sought cover. The outlaw was bound and determined to create more of a ruckus. Why didn't he leave town?

"Ain't a doc within twenty miles. Harrison's Crossing's damned near a ghost town now that the railroad's bypassed us. Ain't nuthin' here to keep folks around, 'cept a ranch or two."

"Quit talking," Slocum ordered. He got his arm around the man's shoulders and half dragged him back toward the empty store.

Now that the man had pointed it out, Slocum saw that most of the buildings were empty. He had been coming through from Dillon on his way to Idaho Falls and hadn't seen anything more than the Shot o' Whiskey Saloon. He had gone in for a drink and found himself in the card game more than an hour back. Sightseeing on the way inside had been limited.

"Might not have a marshal either." The man coughed and wiped blood from his lips. "Heard tell he was thinkin' on leavin' for Pocatello. Has family there."

"Is Idaho Falls the closest town likely to have a saw-bones?"

"And a vet. And 'bout ever'thing else I'm gonna need. Like an undertaker. You see I get a proper burial, will you, mister?"

"You're not that badly shot up," Slocum said. He pulled back the man's shirt and tried to decide if he meant it. From the way the bullet had gone clean through, he probably did mean it. "Press down hard, front and back."

"Hurts like hell."

Slocum started to offer his opinion of what it would feel like dead when he heard movement at the rear of the building. He brought up his six-shooter, ready to shoot.

"One moment, sir. Don't fire!"

Slocum frowned as the tall, well-built man stepped from

the shadows. He wore fancy duds that cost more than Slocum had ever earned in a year as a cowboy. A flashy plum-colored velvet coat hung perfectly tailored over a gold brocade vest. Stiffly starched white ruffles billowed up at the throat like on some European prince. The man's beige pants were a tad tight, and he wore shiny shoes instead of boots. All that kept Slocum from gunning him down was the way he held out his empty hands in front of him. That and his companion.

Stepping from behind was about the loveliest woman Slocum had seen in a month of Sundays. She wore her raven-dark hair tucked under a bonnet. Her dress rivaled that of the man's clothing in cost and style. Her pale face glowed with an intense inner light that almost lit up the dark interior. Ebony eyes fixed boldly on him, daring him—to do what? Where the man's hands were empty, she clutched a notebook and a pencil.

"You a reporter?" Slocum asked.

"Ain't a paper in Harrison's Crossing. Ain't been for danged near a year," the wounded man got out. "If she'd been a reporter, the paper'd never have folded. Folks woulda bought a copy just to see her."

"I am Mr. Randolph's amanuensis," she said, using her pencil like a spear to stab at Slocum. Then she hastily scribbled something in the notebook.

"What the hell's that?"

Slocum and the wounded man had spoken simultaneously. He had to laugh, in spite of the man's condition.

"What *is* that?" Slocum repeated.

"Sir," she said, fixing him with her direct gaze, "I am recording the life and times of the world's greatest writer, Mr. Rory Randolph."

"Him? He's Rory Randolph? Never heard of him."

"Am I to assume you have never heard of Will Stringfellow either?"

"Can't say that I have." Slocum cast a quick look over his shoulder back into the street. "Is it Stringfellow who killed the man in the saloon and wounded him?" He pointed to the man sitting on the dirty floor, trying to keep from bleeding to death.

"It certainly is, sir," Randolph said. His voice boomed, bass and resonant, in the empty room. "He is the most notorious outlaw west of the Big River."

"And north of the Missouri," the woman added.

"Yes, and north of the Missouri. I have come to record his dastardly deeds." Randolph paused and scowled. "It was made more difficult when I realized he knew of me." The man cast a quick, guilty look at the woman. Slocum knew there was more here than they spoke of, but he cared more about the lead flying through the air—and taking the lives of innocent men all around him.

"I don't know about these things," Slocum said, "but if he knew you, wouldn't that make him more inclined to talk?"

Four more slugs tore through the thin wall and drove Slocum forward. His arms circled the woman's trim waist. He lifted and carried her to the floor, out of the line of fire. They came down in a pile, she struggling beneath him.

"Stay down or you'll get yourself ventilated," he said.

"Ventilated? See, Rory, the natives do speak that way."

"I surrender to your superior knowledge, my dear." He bent at the waist to bow.

Arching his back, Slocum reached up, grabbed a handful of ruffles, and yanked hard, bringing the man down to his knees and choking loudly as the fabric tightened around his neck.

"You, too. If this Stringfellow is that mean an hombre, he won't think twice about killing you, too."

Slocum noticed that the woman had stopped struggling and remained quietly under his weight. She looked up at him as if he were a side of beef being judged for quality and weight. He pushed away, sat, then scooted toward the doorway. He poked his six-shooter out and carefully scanned the street, moving from left to right for any sign of the murdering outlaw.

"You tore my ruff."

Slocum looked back at the fancy man. Randolph tried to tuck his torn ruffles back into place.

"You're damned lucky you didn't get your sack blown off," he said. "Keep your head down."

"Are you going after him?" The woman came up behind Slocum, staying on hands and knees, oblivious to the damage done to her expensive dress.

"I would," Slocum said, "but I've got more important things to do."

"There is quite a reward on Stringfellow's head," she said. "Wouldn't a hundred dollars entice you to track him down?"

"I'd do it for nothing," Slocum said. "He shot me and put a couple holes in my Stetson. I paid twelve dollars for this hat." He took off the hat and thrust a finger through the hole in the brim, then moved to the one through the crown.

"Oh, you're injured." She reached out and touched his scalp. His yelp made her pull back abruptly. "I'm sorry. I didn't mean to hurt you further."

"Here," Slocum said, reaching into his pocket for his handkerchief. "Wipe the blood off your fingers."

"I've never seen a man who's been shot before."

"Here's your chance to see one up close."

She started to dab at his scalp but he pushed her away.

"Him. He's the one who needs help." He pointed at the man who had taken Stringfellow's bullet through his gut.

"Oh, yes, of course."

"Do you have a horse? Can you ride?" Slocum asked the wounded man.

"Might be hard for me. Got a wagon out back all hitched up fer these people. I used to run the general store here and was only comin' back to collect a debt from Gus over at the Shot o' Whiskey. Never got that far 'fore . . ."

Slocum didn't see Stringfellow anywhere outside. The outlaw finally had burned through his streak of mean and realized running was better than remaining behind. The wounded shopkeeper looked pale but strong enough for a trip. The woman, for her part, gamely pressed Slocum's handkerchief into the wound, oblivious to the blood. Rory Randolph looked a little green around the gills at the sight of blood but otherwise was unharmed.

"I'll load you into the wagon, get my horse, and we'll head out right away for Idaho Falls. We can make it before nightfall."

"That's pushin' harder than I might be able to tolerate. But settin' 'round jawin' 'bout it's not gettin' me to a doctor."

Slocum slid his six-gun into its holster, lifted the shopkeeper, and went to the back door. He kicked it open, paused to be sure Stringfellow hadn't circled and laid an ambush, then helped the man to the back of the wagon. With a shuddery sigh, the man stretched out on a pile of empty burlap sacks amid crates of supplies that weighed down the wagon something fierce.

"I could go to sleep here and now," he said. "But I still feel all liquid inside, so we'd better get on the road."

"I'll be back in a few minutes," Slocum said after checking the supplies. The wagon carried enough food for a month's trip into the mountains. Nowhere, though, did he find what he sought.

Slocum edged around the building, then went to the saloon, where he had left his horse. The men inside argued over what had happened. Slocum leaned over the bar and grabbed a full bottle of whiskey.

"Medicine," he explained to the barkeep. Before the man could ask for payment, Slocum left.

He stashed the bottle in his saddlebags and rode around to the back of the abandoned store. With a quick cinch, he fastened his pinto's reins to the back of the wagon, then settled down in the driver's box. He started to snap the reins to get the team pulling when he heard sounds behind. He turned, hand going for his six-shooter.

"May I ride with you, sir? Thank you." The woman climbed up and pressed close to him.

"What about him?" Slocum jerked his thumb back toward Rory Randolph.

"He is quite at home in the saddle. This gives him so much more experience to write about."

"You're not coming along."

"If you don't get the team pulling, we'll be here all day long," she said. Her warm hand rested on Slocum's thigh and squeezed down suggestively.

Against his better instincts, Slocum got the two lop-eared mules moving along the road to Idaho Falls, the woman beside him muttering to herself, the wounded man in the wagon bed groaning at every bump in the road, and the dandy riding along behind too far back to be heard. No circus had ever presented a stranger sight.

2

"It's good of you to drive Mr. Merriman like this," the dark-haired woman said. She eyed Slocum boldly, as if daring him to disagree.

"How is it you know his name? I thought you just blundered into the back of the building when the shooting started."

"Oh, no, I hired him. Rather, Mr. Randolph hired him as a guide. Mr. Merriman used to own that store, but when the town went belly up, he relocated to Idaho Falls."

"Then we're taking him home. Good."

"Does that matter to you? That he will be with his people?" She sounded genuinely surprised at the idea.

"I'm not going to care for him. Are you?"

"Why, no, of course not. He is merely an employee. His welfare is of some concern, especially considering how he was shot, but I—Mr. Randolph, that is—have no stake in nursing him back to health."

"He's laid in quite a larder back there," Slocum said, casting a quick glance over his shoulder at the man slumped between the crates. For a moment his and the woman's faces were only inches apart. She didn't move. He did.

"We anticipated a grand hunt that would require a considerable amount of time in the field."

"What were you after?"

"Mr. Randolph wanted to track down the very man who shot up the town. Will Stringfellow. It is quite a coincidence that we found him so quickly and didn't require Mr. Merriman's frontier guidance."

"He's a storekeeper, not a scout."

"You can tell that by looking at him? Fascinating. What are the clues?"

"Pasty face. He spends most of his time indoors. He's not bowlegged so he's not accustomed to riding a horse for weeks on end." Slocum gee-hawed and got the mules pulling in concert. The one on the left balked while the animal on the right kept pulling. They would have turned in circles if he didn't fight them constantly. "More than that, I don't see a rifle or six-shooter anywhere. He's not packing an iron and his right hip's not all shiny from wearing a holster."

"Ah, yes, I understand. The rubbing of a holster against his hip would wear down the cloth. You are quite observant, sir. May I ask your name?"

"John Slocum."

"I am Melissa Benton."

"The amanuensis to the gussied-up dude back there."

"I see that I must be careful what I say and do around you, Mr. Slocum. Your memory is quite extraordinary. Or may I call you John? You don't miss a detail."

"Some I do," he said. "I have no idea what that fancy word means."

"I record things for Rory. He is such a fine writer. In many ways he is like you." She put her hand on his arm to quiet him. "I mean that he is quite expert at what he does, just as you are at your profession. I take you to be a scout. For the cavalry?"

"Done that. Spent the summer wrangling cattle. So you're a secretary?" Melissa bristled a mite at this, then forced herself to relax.

"That is so. I make speaking engagements for him and see that he is there on time."

"Reckon you write what he says, too." This produced an even more pronounced reaction. She scooted away a few inches and stared straight down the road before answering.

"Why do you say that?"

"I've listened to snake oil salesmen and barkers of all kinds. Randolph doesn't have their gift of gab. He couldn't convince me to take a drink of cool water if I'd been in the desert for a week."

"His speeches leave something to be desired, but he is a tremendously talented writer. His books sell thousands of copies."

"Why were you after Stringfellow? From everything I've seen, he's a cold-blooded killer and not the sort to spill his guts to the likes of Randolph."

"Oh, men such as Stringfellow might begin as close-mouthed and suspicious, but with proper incentives, they willingly tell of their adventures. They want to be known. They want the fame being in one of Rory's books can bring them. Trust me on this. I know. I've seen it many times."

"Then Randolph steals their stories and makes a fortune off selling them?"

Melissa laughed, but little humor came through what should have been a musical sound.

"You have such a delightfully primitive way of expressing yourself, John. Outlaws such as Stringfellow would be unknown if it weren't for writers like Rory popularizing their exploits."

"You said that Stringfellow's got a reward on his head. The right people know all about him."

"Do you mean the law? We will certainly interview any marshal who captures such a notorious outlaw. That would be an exciting part of the saga, virtue triumphing over lawlessness."

"I've been in these parts for close to seven months and I never heard of Will Stringfellow before today. That's not too notorious."

"He has fled from crimes committed farther east, where he is *very* well known. We rode up the Missouri in a riverboat, then took the train northward in our hunt for him. I can say without question Stringfellow's exploits are the most popular of any Rory has written."

Slocum let that roll around in his head as he worked the mule team. The road turned increasingly rocky. Avoiding the larger stones made an easier ride in the back for the wounded man. Slocum kept an ear cocked for Merriman's occasional moans that let him know life still pulsed through the veins. The steepness of the incline and the slowness of the mules began to eat away at Slocum. It wasn't possible to get Merriman to Idaho Falls today. They were heading due south and the sun had already dipped behind distant mountains, threatening twilight in a matter of an hour. Even a second day on the road might not be long enough.

"What are you thinking, John? You have a pensive look."

"He's not getting any better, and the town's a ways off. I might ride on into Idaho Falls and fetch the doctor to save your guide the rest of the trip. Being bounced around back there's not doing him any good."

"What? You'd leave us alone out on the prairie?" The outrage from the writer startled Slocum.

He looked to his left. He hadn't noticed Rory Randolph riding so close that he overheard everything being said.

"We'd be sitting ducks out here." The expression on Randolph's face would have been comical if there hadn't been such a hint of pure panic mixed in with the outrage.

"I've heard of some Cree Indians in the area. They were run off their land up in Canada and are waiting for the chance to sneak back north. I don't see them as a problem."

"Indians? Redskins *and* outlaws? You can't leave us like that, not with an injured man who might die at any moment."

Slocum started to tell the writer what he thought about his attitude, but Melissa put her hand on his arm and silenced him.

"Rory is understandably uneasy." Louder, to the writer, she said, "It will be all right. Mr. Slocum simply voiced a possible way of saving Mr. Merriman some pain. The journey is quite tiring for a man in his condition, you realize."

"Yeah, I know." Randolph leaned over and peered down at the shopkeeper. "He's strong enough to make it into town."

Slocum let the author and his secretary debate how long their hired hand would last on the trail. He kept his eyes fixed on the horizon and a suspicious dust cloud that worked its way from east to west. With the wind blowing from the north giving them a tailwind, that meant a sizable party of riders crossed the road a couple miles ahead of them. Stringfellow had been alone back at Harrison's Crossing. The Cree he had mentioned to Melissa were a more likely cause of so much commotion.

The Indians had no fight with anyone in the area that Slocum had heard. The rancher he had worked for through the summer had good relations with the small band and had given them a few head of cattle when they weren't able to hunt any buffalo. That didn't mean the riders in the distance were Cree or any other tribe. They might be cavalry. Or they might be outlaws. Slocum let out a sigh as he considered what to do. He finally asked Melissa the question festering in his head.

"You said Stringfellow is a wanted outlaw. Is he a loner or does he have a gang?"

"Why, I don't know. What do you think, Rory?"

The writer trotted closer. Slocum looked from the man to the woman and back. He felt as if they were playing a game of tag with him, casting knowing looks back and forth. Melissa played it coy, waiting for her boss to supply an answer she already knew.

"He's got a fair-sized band of ruffians riding alongside," Randolph said.

"A dozen or so?"

"Perhaps that many, though I have heard rumors of only half that. Why do you ask?"

The dust cloud had vanished. If the riders kept moving west, they might cut across country and go directly to Idaho Falls. The road was still heading close to due south, but it had to bend eventually to the southwest to reach the town.

"No reason." Slocum hunched over as a new gust of wind at his back turned colder. Melissa snuggled closer and once more rested her hand on his thigh. He wasn't sure what he thought of that with a wounded man in the back and her boss riding a few yards away.

"Don't worry. Rory won't notice."

"We've got to camp for the night," Slocum said suddenly. He straightened when her hand tightened on his leg and moved a bit higher.

"Good," she whispered in his ear. Then Melissa slid away and called out to Randolph that they were camping.

"We have to press on. Staying out here is so . . . primitive."

Slocum snorted at that. Melissa had used the same word to describe him. He had no desire to read any of Randolph's potboilers, but thinking like that made him wonder how cowboys such as himself were portrayed.

"I like the word 'savage' better," Slocum said as he tugged on the reins and tried to convince the mules to do what they had desired all day long. Only now, they wanted to keep pulling the wagon. They were as contrary as any animal Slocum had ever encountered.

"I do, too," Melissa said, looking at him like a wolf eyed its dinner.

"There's a ravine that'll give us shelter from the wind. We might be in for a storm if this wind's any indication."

"Is it safe to camp in a dry wash if you fear a storm will strike?"

"The ravine's wide enough to divert a flood from a major storm. That's not likely, as warm as it's been the past couple weeks. Only now's the weather thinking about winter. Even if it fills, we'll have time to get to higher ground."

"If you say so. I have heard of flash floods," she said skeptically.

She let out a yelp as Slocum bounced over a rock and headed down the gradual incline to the ravine. What she said was true, but protection from the wind counted more to Slocum at the moment. He pulled up near an embankment, fastened the reins to the brake, and hopped down to inspect the harness and yoke, then free the mules so they could graze on some sparse grass growing nearby.

"I hear water running not too far away," he said. "Fetch some so we can fix dinner."

"You want me to get water? I'm the boss, you're the hired hand. You get it, boy."

Slocum started to square off against Randolph, but the man wasn't packing a side arm. He still pushed back his duster to free the Colt resting against his left hip.

"Wait, John," Melissa said anxiously. "Rory didn't mean that the way it sounded."

"He meant it exactly the way it sounded. He's the one who's good with words. He needs to apologize."

"For what?" Rory Randolph dropped to the ground and came over. If he expected to intimidate Slocum with his superior height and bulk, he was mistaken. Even with his chest puffed out and his fists raised, the writer presented no threat to Slocum.

"Rory, go see how Mr. Merriman is doing. I'll talk to Mr. Slocum."

She took Slocum's arm and steered him away from the wagon. Randolph knelt in the back and spoke with the wounded man.

"This is all new and different for him. Forgive him if he doesn't understand everything about the frontier."

"He's not got a good grip on being polite. I don't care that he's a greenhorn. First thing he has to realize is that I don't work for him. Merriman might have, but I don't. I'm seeing a wounded man to a town where a doctor can patch him up. Nothing else."

"Rory sees the world differently than you and me." She kept moving him away. "Where can we find water? I'll help carry it back."

"There's a bucket in the back of the wagon. Get it while I scout for the pond."

"I . . . Very well, John."

Melissa hurried off. He watched as she leaned into the wagon, standing on one leg and bending over a long ways. She presented a fine figure. He even caught sight of an ankle and the woman's calf when a gust of wind blew her skirt up. Melissa looked in his direction, saw his interest, and smiled. Again he had the feeling of prey being hunted. He wasn't sure if being devoured by this huntress was such a bad thing.

She found the bucket and returned.

"Where's the water?" It came as a challenge, as if she thought he had been funning her.

"That way," he said. "Past the bank of the wash. I can smell it."

"Really?" Then she poked him in the ribs with her index finger. "You're joking, aren't you? You can't smell water. This isn't the ocean all filled with salt and fish."

He set off, letting her rush to keep up. He climbed the steeper bank on the far side of the ravine, took her hand and easily pulled her up after him, then said, "See the trees? They're growing around a pond."

"The trees are what you smelled? But—"

She spoke to thin air. Slocum was halfway to the pond. He kept his hand on his pistol as he approached, wary of larger predators having come out to find dinner in the fading light of day. Only the wind soughing through the upper tree branches disturbed the silence.

"Is there something to fear?"

"What do you mean?"

"You look ready to throw down."

Slocum laughed.

"You're sounding like what gets written down in your boss's books." He let his duster fall back down straight. As he turned, he found her pressed warmly against him.

"The wind's cold. Keep me warm, John."

"Would Randolph mind?"

"He won't budge from the wagon. He's not the adventurous type, except in print."

Her arms circled his waist, moving under his duster. She pulled closer so her breasts crushed against his chest. Looking up, her dark eyes twinkled. Her lips parted slightly, she tipped her head back and closed her eyes. What she expected next was obvious.

Slocum didn't disappoint her. Bending down, his lips found hers. The kiss started light, teasingly gentle. Then their passions soared and the kiss deepened. Slocum's tongue slipped out and made a quick circuit, snakelike, across her lips before invading her mouth. Their tongues dueled and darted about, playing hide and seek from one mouth to the other and back. His hands pressed into the small of her back to hold her in place. But she wasn't going anywhere. Her hands behind his back were equally insistent.

Breaking from her lips, Slocum worked across her cheek with fleeting kisses that caused her to gasp. He moved to her arched throat and downward, pulling away at her bodice to expose the soft swell of her perfectly shaped breasts. He lavished kisses on the tops. Using his tongue, he worked farther under the cloth and pressed into a taut nipple. When he did, she sagged. He had to support her weight with his hands.

"I'm weak with need, John. Don't torment me anymore. Please, don't!"

He answered with more kisses. He saw no reason to hurry. The pressure in his jeans mounted as his manhood turned hard. But he wasn't painfully trapped. Not yet. He continued his kissing down into the deep valley between her snowy tits. She knocked off his hat and ran her hands through his lank black hair, guiding his motion now in complete disregard for what she had said only seconds before. Even if he had wanted, he could not escape the sumptuous canyon because of her strong hands pressing him downward.

He felt her body straining. Moving his hands downward, he caught at the twin curves of her ass cheeks. He lifted slightly, bringing her up onto her toes. Every muscle in her body tightened. She moaned with increasing need as he began dragging up her skirt so he could run his fingers over bare flesh on her thighs. Then he slipped his hand between her legs and stroked upward into the fleecy triangle that was already damp with desire.

His finger entered her. She shuddered all over and sagged even more.

"I . . . I can't stand up, John. You make me weak in the knees."

He withdrew his finger from its hot, damp berth. Before she could protest this retreat, he swung her around so she faced away from him. Melissa wasn't lying about how weak she had become. She lost her balance and fell forward. He caught her around the waist and steered her to the right, where she could brace her hands against a stump.

"When I saw you bending over in the wagon to reach the water bucket, I knew what you'd like most," he whispered.

"What, John? What is it I'd like from you?"

He lifted her skirts to reveal the curves of her rump. His hand stroked between her thighs again, moved upward, and parted her legs to allow easier entry from behind. A half step forward, a quick unfastening of his buttoned fly, and he was as ready as the woman for what came next. Hands on her hips to pull her backward, he thrust with an even, easy stroke. The head of his manhood touched the pinkly scalloped lips but did not pause. He pushed through the delicate veil and entered her, inch by inch, slowly, arousing her every desire until he was buried balls deep.

She made tiny incoherent sounds, then began rotating her hips to stir him about in her moist, fleshy cauldron.

Slocum sucked in his breath when she tightened her inner muscles and firmly held him within. Against this he withdrew as slowly as he had entered. They both gasped at the sensations wracking them. When only the purpled arrowhead of his shaft remained within her, he paused, then shoved back into her. This time he moved faster. His balls tightened. Fire grew from embers to a raging forest fire in his loins. His body trembled like a racehorse ready to run. He shoved himself as far into her core as he could.

The exit came faster. The reentry quicker still. Speeding up with every stroke, he was soon burning them both up with the friction of flesh against flesh. Their nerves sang a song of lust and then she cried out, arched her back, and tossed her head so that her long mane of midnight hair floated up and caught on the wind, a banner signifying total sexual release.

Slocum continued to stroke a few more times until he no longer held back the fiery white tide that boiled up and out. Fierce action slowed, then stopped as his lust was spent. When he went flaccid, he stepped back. She looked over her shoulder at him. Her cheeks were flushed as was her neck and the tops of her breasts.

She started to speak, had to catch her breath, and finally gasped out, "You're hired."

"There's not enough money in the world for that. I did what I wanted."

"What we both wanted," she said.

Lowering her skirt, she twisted around and sat on the stump that had supported her hands. She looked up at him, her eyes dewy with sexual hunger only beginning to fade.

"Mr. Merrriman's not going to be able to be our guide, not in his condition. I want to hire you."

"What would Randolph say?"

She sniffed and shook her head.

"He won't object."

"I told you. There's not money enough for that."

"There will be fringe benefits." She lifted one foot to the stump so her skirt slipped back and revealed her bare leg. In the darkness, Slocum had to guess at the patch between her legs. But he didn't have to guess at what she was offering.

Hire on and he got paid money from Rory Randolph and sex from her. It was an enticing offer. He had a few dollars from the poker game and nowhere in particular to go.

"No thanks."

"But—"

Slocum wasn't sure why he turned her down, but he did. As alluring as Melissa was, her boss was trouble waiting to happen.

"Water, then back to the wagon. Your boss is going to be all fidgety if you're gone too long."

"It's not like that between us, John. Between Rory and me."

"You just work for him," he said. "Yeah, sure. But I see the way he looks at you."

"I can handle him. I can keep him in his place."

Slocum filled the bucket and started back to the wagon, not bothering to respond. He had payment enough for doing his good deed shepherding Merriman to Idaho Falls.

He heard Melissa thrashing about in the underbrush behind him, mumbling to herself. He slid down the bank into the ravine, sloshing some water before reaching back to hold out his hand for her. She pointedly ignored him.

Then she tumbled from the bank and crashed into him as gunshots destroyed the silent dusk.

3

Water splashed over them as they rolled, Slocum's arms tight around the woman. Melissa fought, but he clung fiercely to her until he spun behind a large rock. Only then did he release her and struggle to shove his duster out of the way to draw his six-shooter.

"What's going on?" she demanded.

A new flurry of gunfire erupted. This time slugs whined off the ground all around them. Slocum rolled from side to side, got his Colt out, and flopped onto his belly ready to shoot. First he had to figure out what the hell was happening.

Nothing made sense. Rory Randolph sat in the driver's box, his head swiveling back and forth as if it were attached to a Regulator clock pendulum. The mules had run off. The bright flash in the twilight allowed Slocum to home in on the assailant hidden a couple dozen yards along the far ravine rim.

"Who is it? Why's he shooting at us?"

"He's a piss-poor shot," Slocum said, bracing his hand against the ground for extra accuracy. He squeezed off a round. In the dark, he and Melissa were almost invisible. The muzzle flash from his six-shooter gave away their position.

His round missed the sniper by a country mile but drew the man's attention. When Slocum saw only a pinpoint star exploding, he knew he was looking straight down the rifle barrel. The slug tore into the ground a foot in front of him and kicked up a small cloud of dust and rock. He fired again. This time his aim was better, in spite of the range. His shot drove the sniper back.

"Who is it?" Melissa tried to sit up.

Slocum grabbed her arm and brutally yanked her back flat. He said nothing, no matter how she struggled. He fired again when the sniper foolishly outlined himself against the sky, a shadow moving among shadows. This shot found a fleshy target, but Slocum felt in his gut it wasn't a serious wound.

"Don't treat me like this. I demand to know what's going on."

"Stay here," Slocum said.

He dug in his toes and sprinted toward the wagon, where Randolph still swayed from side to side. Slocum slammed into the side of the wagon, then reached up and grabbed a handful of the man's fancy coat. With a heave, he pulled Randolph off the driver's box, and the writer crashed to the ground.

"Are you hit?" Slocum asked.

Randolph gasped to catch his breath. Slocum checked him quickly. The fall and shock had robbed the man of his voice. No blood marred the coat or the fancy ruffled shirt Slocum had ripped up back at Harrison's Crossing. Taking a handful of fabric again, Slocum heaved Randolph up and sat him against a wagon wheel.

"Did you see who shot at you?"

The man shook his head carefully, as if any sudden movement would cause his brains to roll out his ears. For all he had seen of the writer, Slocum wasn't sure how far from reality this was.

He edged around Randolph, then rolled under the wagon,

coming out on the far side, where he could cover any movement along the ravine bank. The wind picked up and masked
small sounds. Slocum stood and chanced a quick look
around. Whoever had shot at them was nowhere to be seen.

He looked into the wagon bed, where Merriman squirmed
about on the burlap.

"You shot?"

"Damned right I am, but that was back in town. I didn't
catch sight of the varmint taking potshots at us now."

Merriman forced himself up out of the canyon between the
crates, got his knees under him, and reared up. Slocum saw
movement, yelled a warning, and fired simultaneously. The
rifleman showed himself not far away. The muzzle flash gave
Slocum a quick look at Stringfellow's ugly face. The man
sneered as he fired a second time, then dived down to avoid
Slocum fanning his Colt in an attempt to drive him away.

"I got to go after him. Are you all right?" Slocum asked
Merriman.

No answer. Slocum glanced toward the last spot where
Stringfellow had fired, then into the wagon bed. Merriman
lay sprawled on his back, his legs bent under him in a way
that would have made any man moan in pain. Any living man.

Slocum reloaded, went to the back of the wagon, and
dropped the gate. He grabbed at Merriman and pulled him
a few feet. Stringfellow's bullet had entered Merriman's
temple but hadn't exited on the other side of the skull. Slocum felt a bit queasy thinking how the bullet had stirred
around in the shopkeeper's brain. The only good thing he
could find in the death was that it had been quick.

"John, is he gone?"

"He's dead," Slocum said, not turning to face Melissa.
"You should have stayed where you had cover."

"But if he's left, what's the danger?"

"I meant Merriman. He's dead. Stringfellow got lucky
with his last shot."

"Dead?" Melissa put her hand on Slocum's shoulder and

lifted herself enough to peer around him at the body. "Oh, no."

"What's wrong? Haven't you ever seen a dead man before?"

She shook her head.

"Go see to your boss. Randolph's by the right front wheel. Don't go wandering out in the middle of the ravine. Stay where you can take cover."

"What are you going to do?"

"Isn't that obvious?" He pushed her in Randolph's direction, then backtracked enough to edge up the slope where he had driven the wagon only an hour earlier.

Once atop the rim, he dropped into low grass and studied the terrain for any sign that Stringfellow had stayed back to get a few more kills. The wind picked up and bent the buffalo grass almost flat to the ground. The only thing Slocum saw moving were the ants beginning to chew away at his hands and wrists. In spite of the insect bites, he stayed stock-still and waited. Finally the distant pounding of a horse's hooves reached his ears. Judging by the direction, Stringfellow was hightailing it.

Moving slowly, Slocum retreated, went back down into the ravine, and found Rory Randolph and his secretary huddled together under the wagon.

"Is it safe to come out?"

"Yeah," Slocum said to the writer. "Stringfellow got in one deadly shot, then cut and ran."

Both Randolph and Melissa eased from their safe spot. The woman hovered between the men, as if drawn—or repelled—by both. She swayed first in one direction then the other, like a reed in the wind, until she came to a halt equidistant from either man.

"You're sure it was the outlaw?" Her voice was steadier than Slocum had expected after all she had been through. "Stringfellow?"

"I saw his face. Not for long but long enough to be

certain." He slid his six-shooter into its holster and wiped his hands on his pants. "Is there a shovel in the wagon?"

"Why do you want a shovel?" Randolph regained his voice. He tried to strike a pose showing how manly he was. Slocum would have laughed if the situation hadn't been so dour. "Well, sir? Answer me."

"To bury Merriman. You go fetch the mules and bring them back. If you're inclined, take them to the pond and let them drink. Melissa can show you the way."

"Act as a liveryman? I should say not." Randolph puffed himself up even more.

"Then you bury him, and I'll take care of the mules. Those four-legged, long-eared balky beasts are your only way to Idaho Falls."

"What about you, John? They're your only way, too," the woman said.

"I've got my horse."

"You can't abandon us out here in the wild," Randolph protested.

"You've got a fine imagination if you write those books about the Wild West. You can think up a way of getting to town by your lonesome."

"Wait, John, Rory. Don't argue." Melissa turned her back on her boss and led Slocum away. "With Mr. Merriman dead, it is imperative that we go to Idaho Falls and let the law know what's happened. You are the only witness to who killed that poor man. Rory and I would be giving what is legally known as hearsay evidence." She clung to his arm and almost pulled him off balance. "More than that, I want to hire you to take Mr. Merriman's place. We need a guide, a man who knows the countryside. That's you, John. I—Rory—can pay very well. Twice what a guide would usually get."

"You don't know how much that is," Slocum said.

"Fifty dollars a month. I'll offer a hundred. Rather, Rory will pay you that princely sum to guide us."

"Guide you to what? You wanted to find Stringfellow.

He's got it in for you and will cut you down like a scythe going through wheat if he sees you."

"I hear hesitation in your voice," she said. "You want to help us out. I told you what extra consideration might be given. It could be quite exciting for you. And there's the chance Rory will see fit to write you into one of his novels. You'll be famous, your name will be recognized all around the world."

That made Slocum a tad uneasy. His past was littered with crimes that put Will Stringfellow to shame. The law had been after him ever since he killed a Reconstruction carpetbagger judge for trying to steal the family farm. Since riding west, he hadn't been an angel. He hadn't even tried. Rory Randolph might bring down the law on his head if he used Slocum's name and description.

"Don't do that," he said.

Melissa got a sly look, smiled just a little, and said, "Help us and I'll see that Rory never mentions you in one of his dime novels. Leave us and . . ." Her words trailed off, and she shrugged eloquently in a way that left no room for misinterpretation.

Slocum regretted having given his real name to the woman now. She used that slip as a lever to blackmail him.

"You and the writer fellow take care of the mules. I'll see to planting the dead man."

She grinned, stood on tiptoe, and gave him a quick kiss. With a spin that sent her skirts whirling outward, she ran to Rory and spoke urgently to him. Slocum watched until he saw Randolph coming around to Melissa's way of thinking. That wasn't much of a surprise. She had wielded her wiles over him for some time, so she knew exactly what arguments to make. She had only met Slocum earlier that day and had learned to similarly beguile him.

As she and Randolph went off into the twilight to find the mules, Slocum pulled Merriman from the wagon and laid him out on the ground. He went through the man's pockets and found a few personal items and ten dollars in silver. He tucked those into his own vest pocket and completed his search. Nothing else showed the man had even been alive.

Unable to find a shovel, Slocum used a slat taken from a crate to scrape away the rocky, sandy soil in the ravine. Burying a man here invited trouble. Come spring runoffs, the body likely would be washed up and carried downstream. Slocum wasn't up to lugging the corpse to a higher elevation and burying it in harder ground. All he wanted was to keep the man's body from being the evening meal for a pack of coyotes. Come spring, only bones would be left to be washed downstream. Whatever happened, it no longer mattered to the shopkeeper.

The last of the rocks piled atop the grave dropped into place when Melissa and Randolph returned with the mules.

"All watered. We let them feed some on the grass by the pond," Melissa said. She looked at the rock cairn. "Is he all taken care of?"

"Reckon so, unless you want to say a few words over the grave." Slocum saw the woman wasn't inclined to do that. "How about you? You're the expert with the words."

Rory Randolph shuffled his feet like a schoolboy caught shooting spitballs in class.

"I don't have anything to say."

"The mules have rested some. I don't like traveling at night, but staying out here is less inviting by the minute. Saddle up. We'll drive straight through to town."

"I can do that," Randolph said, more to Melissa than Slocum. He went off to saddle his horse and step up onto the mare.

Slocum helped Melissa into the driver's box, then climbed after her. He settled down, tired to the bone.

"We can rest in Idaho Falls," she said. "A night in a nice hotel. Then we can decide what to do." Her hand rested on his arm, then squeezed enough to be reassuring and to suggest what more they might do in that hotel with a nice feather mattress and bedsprings.

"Next stop, town," Slocum said. He snapped the reins and got the mules pulling up the slope. It took him longer than he'd expected to find the road and get the wagon wheels settled into the dual ruts.

Melissa chattered gaily for a mile, but Slocum wasn't in any mood to respond. She eventually quieted and within another mile clung to his arm, her head on his shoulder. Somehow she slept, giving him a chance to think what he had to do.

They reached the town a little after sunup.

Melissa came awake, rubbed her eyes, then drew the back of her hand across her lips.

"I so do need to brush my teeth. And a meal. And a bed to sleep in." She looked at Slocum and gave him her sly smile. "Then we can find out if that bed's good for anything more."

"There's a hotel," Slocum said. "I'll leave you and Randolph to get rooms. I'll let the marshal know about Stringfellow."

"Don't be long," she said. From the ground she looked up at him and added, "I'll be waiting."

Slocum touched the brim of his hat, snapped the reins, and convinced the mules to pull the wagon another quarter mile to the marshal's office. The lawman was just opening the jailhouse door when Slocum clanked to a halt. The marshal looked up, a sour expression his face. He spat, then said, "You're not bringin' me good news, are you, mister?"

"Can't say that I am, Marshal." Slocum climbed down, stretched his tired limbs, and followed the youngish lawman inside.

The office was impeccably clean, the floor so spotless Slocum wondered if the marshal ate off it. The lawman sat down behind a large polished oak desk and leaned back. He was hardly out of his teens, if that old, clean-shaven, and with eyes that darted about constantly. Slocum doubted the man missed a thing around him. Old and tired lawmen wanted nothing more than to get through a day with nothing happening. That was how they stayed alive to see another dawn. Younger lawmen had a tendency to go out of their way to crush crime. Enforcing the law was more than a job; it was a religious calling. Slocum hoped none of the wanted posters in a neat pile on the marshal's desk carried his likeness.

A man like this would have memorized every face on those posters.

"Tell me about it. No need to spin a tale of heroics. I know you was a hero and done the right thing and deserve a medal, so cut right to the chase."

Slocum began pulling Merriman's belongings from his pocket. He counted out the silver dollars, then pushed the stack across the desk.

"He was a store owner in Harrison's Crossing, but the town's dried up, and rather than blow away, Merriman— never heard his first name—chose to escort some Easterners around so they could sightsee. He crossed an outlaw by the name of Will Stringfellow. You know of him?"

"I do. Him and his gang held up a stagecoach bound for Pocatello a week back. Blowed in from the Dakota Badlands, or so I heard."

"Stringfellow gunned him down. I chased the outlaw off, buried Merriman, and brought you that for his next of kin, if there are any."

"I'll ask around. I know people in Idaho Falls but not up north." The marshal raked everything into his top desk drawer, then locked it before going on. "Who are the people Merriman was escorting around?"

"A writer and his secretary. They're over at the hotel on Lomax Street."

"Got more 'n one hotel."

"Ask around for whoever's just registered," Slocum said.

"Why not? I'm supposed to be good at findin' out such things. What about you?"

"I've got business."

"Business takin' you out of town?" The marshal fixed him with a gimlet look. "That's good. Real good. I make sure Idaho Falls is nice and quiet."

"It'll stay quiet with me gone," Slocum said.

He stepped into the morning sun, unfastened his horse's reins from the back of the wagon, then stepped up. He had an outlaw to track down and a score to settle. Slocum left town without so much as a backward glance as he headed north to find Stringfellow's trail.

4

Animals had pulled away half the rocks Slocum had piled on Merriman's grave. He stared down at the paw prints on the ground around the area and tried to estimate how many coyotes had come for an easy meal. A pack, maybe ten, was the best he could decide. Riding up had driven off the hungry beasts. He considered taking the time to replace the stones to keep those powerful jaws at bay, but then snapped the reins and got his pinto moving out of the ravine and along the bank.

He saw where he had lain, waiting to take a shot at Stringfellow. From this spot of crushed grass he rode directly toward a stand of scrubby oak trees. The trail left by the outlaw had been obscured by a night of strong wind, but Slocum found a broken twig on a low-growing bush and then saw the faint prints in the dirt leading off toward the foothills. Slocum checked his Winchester to be sure it was loaded, then put his heels to his horse's flanks and trotted away. Stringfellow had a day's lead on him.

Slocum homed in on the most likely destination. A deep notch in the hills led deeper into the mountains. If

Stringfellow and his gang were holed up back there, the law needed a huge posse to ever root them out. From what he had seen in Idaho Falls, the town marshal wasn't inclined to do more than keep the peace in his town. Slocum hadn't bothered inquiring after the sheriff or even if a federal marshal roamed the territory. Out here in the wild, law was a scarce commodity.

Usually, the lack of lawmen suited him just fine. Now he wanted a deputy or two at his side. Stringfellow had been alone in Harrison's Crossing, but the marshal had mentioned a gang robbing a stagecoach. Slocum rode after a man who might have a half-dozen guns backing him up. Such odds didn't deter him, but Slocum worried over the purpose of shooting down Stringfellow. Bringing Merriman's killer to justice was the province of the law, but Slocum felt an obligation since no one else was going after Stringfellow. He had promised Merriman he would see him to a doctor, and the outlaw had killed him before they had reached Idaho Falls.

More than this, he had an abiding curiosity as to what interest the outlaw might have in Rory Randolph—or vice versa. No matter what Melissa thought, he wasn't hiring on to nursemaid her boss as he toured the West.

Thought of the woman distracted him for almost a mile, then Slocum drew rein and stood in the stirrups, focused on a canyon branching away from the main trail. Echoes drifted to him from beyond a bend. Horses. Men yelling. He waited for the sounds of gunshots but they never came, and the furor died down.

He studied the rocky walls and cursed. They were steep. The canyon was only a hundred feet or so from floor to rim, but the sheer walls defeated any attempt to ride to the top. Some sections might be climbable, but leaving his horse behind was not in the cards. He had become attached to the sturdy horse over the past six months. The rancher he had worked for supplied every wrangler with a dozen horses, but Slocum and the pinto had found a bond. It wasn't as fast as most of the other horses in the remuda but had always kept slogging along, no matter how tired. When he had parted company with the rancher, he had bought the pinto at an absurdly low price. It was another way for the rancher to reward him for the work he had done over the summer.

He wasn't going to leave the horse behind just to spy on whoever caused the ruckus. Pressing on in the narrow confines of the canyon was dangerous if this was Stringfellow's gang. The outlaw might have posted a sentry to warn of intruders. Where the canyon led was something of a mystery, too, since a decent two-rut road along the floor showed constant travel by heavy wagons. Slocum saw no trace of mining that might require such a road. No tailings spewed forth from the mouths of mines, either active or abandoned. All he could guess was that ranchers used the road to get from one side of the low mountains to the other.

The amount of horse flop along the road made this more likely, but Slocum couldn't tell for certain. Why would an outlaw gang hide along the road unless they intended to waylay ranchers and steal herds of horses being moved to a higher pasture?

Slocum worked off the road and rode as close to one rocky wall as he could. This provided scant protection from being seen by a sentry on the far side of the canyon but gave a little cover if Stringfellow's guard was on the wall above him. He rounded the bend in the canyon and saw how the walls opened out into a grassy valley perfect for grazing small herds. Some distance away a small shack had a half-dozen horses tethered around it.

He had found the outlaws.

All Slocum had to do now was decide what he wanted. Cutting down Stringfellow for killing Merriman ranked high on his list, but what of the men riding with him? Slocum had no quarrel with them.

Keeping a sharp lookout, Slocum edged into the valley. Stringfellow hadn't bothered posting a sentry. Slocum rode into a small stand of trees and tethered his horse. He then scouted the area, found the stream where those in the cabin fetched their water, and settled down. Less than an hour later, two men followed the muddy trail from the cabin to the stream. While one filled a pair of buckets, the other relieved himself against a tree.

"You think we oughta go along with this?"

The man struggling with the filled water buckets put them down and rubbed his hands as he thought about his partner's question. He finally said, "He's sure got a bug up his ass over that writer fellow."

"What's in it for us?" The man finished his business and buttoned up as he went to the stream to sample the water. He sucked loudly, then said, "The stage was a good plan. I wouldn't mind doin' more of that. And a railroad heist could make us all nigh on rich."

"If you call twenty dollars apiece from the stagecoach a good plan."

"It's more 'n we'd get kidnapping that dude." The man chuckled. "If his lady friend is part of the deal, count me in. Even sloppy seconds'd be mighty fine with a filly like that."

"Will's not talkin' about kidnapping. He wants to put the writer six feet under."

"Six feet? Naw, he wants to leave the carcass out for the wolves."

Each hefted a bucket and returned to the cabin. Slocum followed, moving as silently as a shadow through the woods. The two vanished into the cabin. From the smells coming from the chimney, they were fixing supper. Slocum's belly rubbed up against his spine, reminding him how long it had been since he'd eaten. There would be plenty of time for that after he took care of Stringfellow. With a few quick steps he reached the side of the cabin, knelt, and began prying loose mud used to caulk between the logs.

He pressed his eye against the wood and tried to make sense of what he saw inside. It took a little more work to widen the crack. This let him see four men sitting around a table. Another worked at a pot dangling in the flames contained by the fireplace. Slocum hunted for Stringfellow but couldn't spot him.

Then he realized why. He was shoved hard against the cabin wall and narrowly avoided being buffaloed. The instant he hit the ground, he rolled and came up with his six-shooter firing. Will Stringfellow jerked away. Slocum had missed. Then the fight got serious. Stringfellow turned his pistol around and used it as a six-shooter instead of a club.

The air filled with billows of white gun smoke, and dust kicked up as Slocum thrust about, fighting to get to his feet. Stringfellow backed away, still firing. His six-gun came up empty at the same instant Slocum's did.

The exchange had alerted the outlaws inside the cabin, but Slocum knew escape lay in capturing Stringfellow, not in running. He dived forward as the gang leader slipped around the corner of the building. His fingers closed on the man's leg. He hung on for dear life and was dragged along a couple feet before Stringfellow lost his balance and crashed flat on his back. He tried kicking Slocum in the belly, but desperation gave Slocum strength.

He caught the foot and twisted savagely, rolling Stringfellow over. Slocum dropped down, the foot still captive in his armpit. He felt muscles in the outlaw's leg protest and tear. Then strong hands pulled him away.

He hadn't expected the men inside to come boiling out this fast. Slocum kicked and twisted and even got his Colt yanked free, only to remember that it was empty when pulling the trigger resulted only in a dull click.

"Hold that son of a bitch," Stringfellow growled. He kicked away, tried to stand and fell when his injured leg betrayed him. "He busted my damned leg!"

"You want us to kill him, Will? Might be fun letting him run and then hunting him down."

"Shut up, Larry. You ain't got the sense God gave a goose."

"Why're you sayin' shit like that, Will?"

"Because we don't know why he's here, that's why. He's not a lawman. Who sent him?"

"What's the difference?" Larry glowered.

"You always let him talk to you like that, Larry?" Slocum stopped struggling and tried to foment some discord he could turn to his own benefit. All he could do now was escape, but with two men hanging on to his arms and his six-gun empty, he was fast running out of luck.

"He's tryin' to split us up, Larry," the outlaw's leader said. "Don't listen to him." Stringfellow hobbled over and got a better look at his captive. "I'll be damned. This is the galoot I tried to shoot in town. I'm not sure but I think he was the one with the writer when I tried to kill him at the empty store and then later in the gully."

"Then we can kill him. Let me plug him, Will."

Slocum saw that Stringfellow considered this. Larry had shown too much rebellion. If he sacrificed Slocum and any information he might get from him, Stringfellow kept his control of the gang intact. But that didn't answer his questions, ones that might reflect on the gang's chances for staying out of jail. Slocum might be a scout for the cavalry or someone hired by the sheriff or a federal marshal intent on bringing justice to Idaho.

The outlaw shoved his face within inches. Slocum saw how nearsighted Stringfellow was.

"Who sent you? You a deputy?"

"You worried that the marshal over in Idaho Falls had a posse on your trail? I didn't have any trouble finding you. He won't either."

"Get ready to move out, boys," Stringfellow said. "We can't take the risk he's not tellin' the truth."

"Listen to him, Will. He's lyin' through his teeth."

Larry came over and took a swing at Slocum. The blow missed by a fraction of an inch but grazed his cheek. The impact still snapped his head back. The tickle of blood running from a cut made him laugh. It got him a second punch to the face.

"So if he's lyin', that means he don't matter." Stringfellow rubbed his leg and got circulation back. He flexed it at the knee, then kicked Slocum hard in the crotch.

Seeing the kick coming, Slocum lifted one leg enough to block the worst of the kick. It still rattled his teeth and doubled him over. The man holding his arms pulled him erect again.

"What's it gonna be, Will?"

"We hightail it. I got plans for robbin' a train that's gonna have us all knee deep in clover."

"What about him?" Larry drew his six-gun and shoved it into Slocum's mouth.

The taste of steel and gunpowder made Slocum gag. The outlaw pulled the gun back enough to press it against Slocum's forehead.

"Let me kill him. What do you have to say about that?"

"It's been a while since you cleaned your six-shooter," Slocum said. "I didn't taste any gun oil."

For an instant, Larry was taken aback. Then he drew back his gun to crush Slocum's skull. Stringfellow caught his henchman's wrist to prevent it.

"Get your gear. We're clearin' out right now."

"It's almost dark, Will. We'll get lost if we leave now."

"Good. That means anybody on our trail'll get turned around, too." Stringfellow motioned for the men holding Slocum to drag him away from the cabin.

Slocum heard the gate open on the outlaw's six-shooter, then snap shut after six more cartridges had been loaded. At every step he expected a shot to the back of his head.

"Here's good," Stringfellow said. "Stake him out."

Slocum was shoved to the ground and pinned by the two outlaws. As Stringfellow held a gun on him, the two worked to drive stakes into the ground. In less than ten minutes, rope had been found and tied securely around his wrists and ankles. He stared past Stringfellow into the blue sky turning pink with sunset.

It was likely the last sunset he would ever see.

"Go on, boys. Get saddled up. Be sure my horse is ready so we can skedaddle."

The two left, whispering about all the tortures Stringfellow was going to inflict on his captive.

Slocum squinted. Stringfellow moved so the sun was directly behind his head and Slocum could barely see his face, cast in shadow.

"Why are you on my trail? Was it the stagecoach robbery?"

"You shot me for no reason back in Harrison's Crossing."

"I thought you was somebody else." Stringfellow peered at him. "There's more to it than that. Why are you so determined to come after me?"

"Merriman," Slocum said. "I promised to get him to Idaho Falls and a doctor and you shot him down. He was so weak he could hardly sit up, much less use a gun."

"Don't know any Merriman." Stringfellow paused, then said, "That cuss in the wagon back in the ravine? Him the same one from Harrison's Crossing?"

Slocum said nothing.

"He a relative? I'm sorry 'bout him. I was aimin' at the damned writer."

"What's your beef with him?"

"You're not the law, but you got me in your sights. I didn't know this Merriman and didn't want him dead. Rory Randolph, I'd fill with lead, reload, and start all over, the son of a bitch."

"Why?"

Stringfellow bent low until his face was close to Slocum's. Something fell from his pocket, but Stringfellow paid no heed. He was too intent on Slocum.

"I ain't got time to argue the point. I apologize about killin' Merriman and I mistook you fer somebody else in the saloon. That's all you get. If you don't die out here, you get on back to Idaho Falls or wherever you call home and stay there. Forget you ever saw me."

Slocum started to tell Stringfellow how Randolph had hired him, then bit back the taunt when the outlaw pointed his pistol square at his head.

"See you in hell."

Will Stringfellow pulled the trigger.

5

Slocum flinched as the bullet tore past his ear. He hardly heard Stringfellow as he backed off because of the ringing in his ears, but the intent was clear. The only way he would stay alive was to give up tracking down the outlaw. At that instant, Slocum would have strangled the man with his bare hands for staking him out and then deafening him with the pistol shot.

He blinked and got some of the fiery powder residue from his eyes. By the time his vision had cleared, the sky had turned dark enough for stars to pop out. Slocum caught sight of the evening star and made his wish. Then he began tensing and relaxing to work free the stakes holding his arms. When his shoulders began to knot with strain, he knew these stakes were too secure. His shifted his efforts to his legs. Stronger than his arms or the stakes weren't as deeply sunk, he achieved almost immediate success. His right leg flopped free. With considerable twisting and tugging, he got his left leg free in another minute.

From here it was only a matter of straining and pulling before his right hand yanked out the stake and he was free. Using the peg still attached to his right wrist, he dug around

45

the stake on his left and then sat up, completely free of Stringfellow's imprisonment. He rubbed circulation back into his tingling hands, discarded the rope, and got to his feet. His wish on the evening star had come true.

As he took a step, he kicked a small book. He remembered something falling from the outlaw's pocket. Slocum held up the book and peered at it in the growing light from the stars.

A smile curled his lips. Stringfellow had dropped one of Rory Randolph's potboilers.

Backshooting Badman of the Badlands. Slocum had to laugh at it, then flipped open the dime novel to the first page and made out the words. A low whistle escaped his lips.

He saw why Stringfellow had it in for the writer now. In less than a page, Randolph made Stringfellow out to be a mother-murdering, sister-raping madman. If Randolph hadn't mentioned the outlaw by name and given a fair description, including the hooked nose and scar over his eye, Slocum might have put this off as coincidence, but the entire book must have been filled with terrible crimes all laid at Stringfellow's door.

If such a novel had been penned about Slocum, he would be intent on ventilating the author, too.

He tucked the book into his pocket and walked to where he had left his pinto. The horse was gone. Resting his hand on his empty holster, Slocum knew more than the horse had to be retrieved. If he had ever entertained the notion of letting Stringfellow ride off, that was gone now. Stealing a man's six-shooter was one thing, but taking his horse was another.

Slocum went back to the cabin and dropped to his hands and knees. The moon poked up above the mountains to the east, giving him a fair amount of light to work under. When he had the direction taken by the gang, he started walking. The moonlight allowed him to avoid stepping into marmot burrows or holes and breaking his damn fool neck, but he still stewed as he went. He might not work for Rory Randolph, but he always ended up doing what the man would have paid him for. Catching Stringfellow and bringing him in to the law made for a stirring story. He touched the novel in his pocket. It lacked the lurid detail Randolph had put into the first few pages of the book about Stringfellow, but Slocum didn't doubt the writer was up to making it more dramatic than it likely was.

Still, being staked out, having a gun fired in his face, Stringfellow's warning, the theft of his six-shooter and horse, all those were better than any of the rubbish in the book. They were true, not made up.

Slocum had crossed the meadow and entered the woods on the far side when he heard arguments raging ahead. He picked up his pace and moved within a dozen feet of the two outlaws who had held him down and staked him out for Stringfellow.

"Damned shame your horse pulling up lame like that," one said. "I happen to have a spare horse. For a price, I'll rent him to you."

"Rent him? You stole that son of a bitch's horse, and you're offering your swayback nag to me as a temporary? You ought to give me the horse to take it off your hands."

Slocum moved around and caught sight of the two. Both were dismounted. Three horses stood nearby. One favored its right front hoof. It might have thrown a shoe or gotten a stone between its shoe and hoof. Whatever the cause, the outlaw couldn't ride it. But the other horse he had asked for was hardly a swayback. Slocum ignored it as he immediately spotted his paint.

"I ain't got enough money on me. I lost the loot from the stage robbery to Stringfellow."

"He cheated you at cards," said the other. Slocum imagined his smirk. "But I'll show what a great friend I am. Take my spare horse."

"Do tell," the other outlaw said suspiciously. "What do you want?"

"A quarter of your take from the next robbery."

"It might not be much."

"Or it might be like Will says. We can each see a thousand dollars."

"That horse ain't worth two hundred fifty bucks!"

"Might be we get a handful of mail that's worthless. I'm takin' a risk."

The man with the lame horse eventually agreed, grabbed the reins of the other's horse, and swung into the saddle.

"You have to deal with the lame horse. I'll meet you in camp," he said. Before the man riding Slocum's pinto could answer, he galloped away.

The outlaw laughed, mounted, and tugged at the lame horse's reins. From the way it limped along, he wouldn't be able to make very good time. Until he found the cause of the lameness, he wasn't about to shoot the horse. Slocum cut through the woods, got ahead of the rider on the trail, and clambered up a tree. He was wiping sap from his hands when the man rode beneath him.

Not wasting a second, Slocum gripped a limb with both hands and swung down. He planted both feet squarely on the man's chest and kicked like a mule. The outlaw went flying. Slocum had a moment's scare when his hands slipped from the branch and he crashed down. He hit the saddle and then slid off the pinto to land on the ground. Managing to twist in midair like a cat, he hit the ground on hands and knees.

He got to his feet and pivoted, ready to take out the outlaw only to find the man already had his wits back. The outlaw made the mistake of going for Slocum's Colt Navy tucked into his gun belt rather than drawing his own iron holstered at his side. The hammer caught on his vest. Fabric ripped as he yanked harder, but in doing so, the pistol flew upward and away from the intended target.

A quick punch to the man's face unbalanced him. The gun discharged, forcing Slocum to grab for the man's wrist to keep him from swinging it back around and using it as a club. Together they stumbled through the woods until the outlaw's heel caught a rock. They went down in a heap, with Slocum atop him.

For an instant they stared at each other. A slow realization of who pinned him down came over the outlaw. By then Slocum pounded his right fist down on the top of the man's head like he hammered nails while he clung to the man's gun hand with his left. The first blow brought out a cry of pain. The second a moan. The third knocked him out.

Panting, Slocum pried the Colt free of the outlaw's grip. Before getting off him, Slocum plucked the man's gun from its holster. Only then did he stand and look around for his horse. The pinto stood quietly not ten feet away, watching the curious human ritual of fighting. The lame horse hadn't bothered running off—or stumbling away.

Slocum went to the lame horse and soothed it, then lifted its hoof for a quick examination. As he had thought, the horse had a stone under its shoe. Using his knife, he pried it free, then used the butt of the outlaw's pistol to hammer back the nails. The shoe wasn't firmly attached, but the horse no longer limped.

"Larry, help me, Larry!"

The outlaw struggled to sit up as he called out for his partner. Slocum walked to him, leading the horse. Using the loose ends of the reins, he whipped the man across the face.

"Mount up. We're riding."

"I ain't goin' nowhere with you."

Slocum leveled his six-gun, cocked it, and said, "Fine by me."

"Wait, wait, I give up. Don't shoot."

Slocum watched the man mount. Only then did he swing up onto the paint. He silently pointed the way they had come through the forest.

"Would you have gunned me down in cold blood?"

Slocum's silence gave the outlaw more of an answer than simple words.

They reached Idaho Falls by noon the next day. Slocum wanted to ride faster, but the outlaw's horse was pulling up lame again.

"There's the marshal's office," Slocum said, pointing.

"Go to hell."

"I'm heading there someday, but you'll be waiting for me," Slocum said. He rested his hand on the ebony butt of his six-gun. "Get down."

He waited for the outlaw to obey, then swung down and stepped around his horse. He had his six-shooter out and pointed. The man had intended to slug Slocum when he wasn't expecting it.

"Marshal, I've got a visitor for your back cell," Slocum bellowed.

This brought the young marshal running out, his hand on his own pistol. He looked from Slocum to the outlaw, then grinned crookedly.

"As I live and breathe, if it ain't Little Joe Barkhausen. You caught yourself a little fish, but I'm not letting you throw him back."

"He rode along with Stringfellow when they robbed the stage. From what I overheard, they're planning another robbery sometime soon. Might be your prisoner—Little Joe, you called him?—can give you all the details."

"I ain't snitchin' on my friends."

"If I put him in a cell and go for dinner, you think you can look after him?" The marshal looked significantly at Slocum.

"If you're gone long enough."

"A man gets mighty hungry in a town like this. You think an hour's long enough? Or are two better?"

"Wait, don't leave me with him. I'll tell you what you want to know, Marshal. But don't leave him alone with me."

The marshal lifted an eyebrow. "Now why is it he's so skittish around you?"

"Might be something to do with him and his partner staking me out to die, then stealing my horse and gun."

"Get on in there," the marshal ordered, herding the prisoner ahead of him. He thrust out his arm to keep Slocum from going inside, too. "No call for you to spook him none. Unless I miss my guess, his tongue's all loose and flapping now."

"Is there a reward on his head?"

"Twenty-five dollars. I'll see that you get it."

"Is there a blacksmith around town?"

"Down the street a couple blocks, turn south, and Henderson's Shoeing Shop is not far."

"Give him the reward money for shoeing the horse."

The marshal started to ask, then clamped his mouth shut. He had bigger fish to fry if the Stringfellow gang planned a new robbery. Slocum led the horse to the smithy and told the farrier how to expect payment. Whatever happened, the horse would be well cared for. The outlaw might be convicted. If he was, Slocum had a claim on the horse. With any luck, he could sell it for fifty dollars. That was reward enough for risking his life going after Stringfellow.

He stepped out of the blacksmith's forge, thinking hard. He had forgotten about the outlaw leader in the rush to lock up his henchman.

Deciding what to do now presented him with something of a problem. Good sense dictated that he forget what Stringfellow had done to him and ride on. He'd been intent on getting far enough south before winter clutched at the Bitterroots so that all he'd see for weeks on end would be snow. Down El Paso way, the tequila flowed faster than the Rio Grande and the snow was sparse.

"Mr. Slocum."

He jolted out of his reverie to see Melissa Benton standing in the center of the street, her balled hands on her hips.

She glared at him with such intensity he didn't need a shot of tequila to keep warm all winter long.

"Howdy, Melissa."

"Is that all you have to say for yourself? I was so worried about you."

"Do tell." Slocum doubted that.

"So was Rory. He was certain he had lost another employee to that terrible Will Stringfellow."

"The one he wrote about in this here book?" Slocum took *Backshooting Badman of the Badlands* from his pocket and held it up. "This is why Stringfellow wants Randolph's scalp, isn't it?"

"Where'd you get that?"

"Doesn't matter." He tucked it back into his pocket. "I can't blame Stringfellow too much for getting mad after seeing this pack of lies."

"It's true," she said, scowling. "Well, it could be true. Some of it."

"Randolph made it all up and used Stringfellow's name."

"He saw a wanted poster and got his likeness. The rest, well, the rest is a work of fiction."

"Why'd he come out here? To lord it over Stringfellow? That's a mighty dumb thing to do. Stringfellow might not be the best-known outlaw but he's not the meekest one either. Just since our paths crossed, he's killed a couple men and damned near killed me."

"John, really? Tell me about it. What did he do? Don't leave out any details."

Melissa came to him, looped her arm through his, and pulled him close.

"You must be starved. I'll buy you a meal. You can tell me what Stringfellow did. Oh, this is going to be fine!"

He wasn't so sure, but she was a pretty woman, determined, and she had offered him the first decent meal in a week.

6

"Rory needs you," Melissa Benton said. She leaned forward and took his hand in both of hers, squeezing warmly. "*We* need your expertise to keep out of serious trouble."

"Go home," Slocum said. He pulled free of her grip and picked up a cup of coffee potent enough to strip the hair off cowhide. The rest of the meal had been equally bad, but he didn't care. It had been too long since he'd had any food at all. Working the range all summer long had been a treat because the range cook had been better than good at his trade. In spite of long hours in the saddle and backbreaking work, Slocum had put on weight from the tender steaks, the fluffy biscuits, and the fruit pies prepared around the clock.

"Do you really want to get rid of me, John? We can explore so much more than the countryside."

"Why'd Randolph even come out here?" He saw the flash of irritation on Melissa's lovely face and knew whatever she said would be only partly true, if that.

"Research. I told you that."

"Stringfellow is pissed off at him for what he wrote. Randolph didn't pull all that detail out of thin air."

"Writers are imaginative," she said.

"Why Stringfellow? Why name him?"

"He sent a letter to Rory about how much he hated a novel he'd read. Who would have thought an outlaw could read?"

"So Randolph got even by saying all the vicious things in another book? Then sent it to Stringfellow?"

"He never sent a copy to the outlaw. He just found it. Stringfellow didn't like *Red River Rogues* and had the gall to send a wanted poster along with the letter to prove how much he knew and how little Rory did."

Slocum shook his head in wonder. Stringfellow had bragged to the writer about being a real outlaw and probably had pointed out everything wrong in the prior book. A war of words had brought Randolph from New York to call out Stringfellow. That couldn't end well for a man whose idea of west was New Jersey.

"You'll make Stringfellow into a desperado as notorious as Billy the Kid. Is that what you want?"

"It can't hurt either of us."

"Unless Stringfellow adds to his reputation by killing Rory. You don't want a scout. You want a bodyguard, and I won't do that. I never have and never will."

"You brought in one of his gang and turned him over to the marshal. Stringfellow tried to kill you—torture you! You owe him."

"Owe him?"

"Revenge, John, you have to bring Stringfellow to justice to get even. Why, he shot you!" She reached out to touch the healing wound on his scalp.

Slocum saw how she tried to maneuver him around to doing what her boss wanted. There was more than a kernel of truth in what she said. His ear still rang from the muzzle blast when Stringfellow had him tied to the ground and had fired to scare him off. He wasn't the kind to scare, but he wasn't the kind to forgive and forget being shot. But being used by the woman and her employer rankled, too.

But was it being used if he did what he wanted and it matched what Melissa wanted from him?

He finished the last of the poor meal and downed the coffee in a single gulp so he wouldn't have to taste it. The acid drink burned at his gut. He knew it might have been something else tying him up in knots.

"He won't get by with what he did to me," Slocum said.

"Oh, wonderful, John, I knew I could count on you!" She tugged on his hand to hold him in place as she leaned across the table to give him a kiss that drew the unwanted attention of others in the restaurant. One woman sniffed and said something to her husband, who looked away from such a disgusting display of affection in public.

Melissa settled back and brushed off crumbs from the meal that had caught on her blouse. She looked up at him and smiled wickedly.

"Would you like to lick off the morsels?"

"They wouldn't lick off," Slocum said. Melissa laughed boisterously, garnering more angry scowls. "I've got to talk to the marshal."

"You and Marshal Lennox are going after Stringfellow? When? I need to be sure Rory and I have horses and the proper supplies."

"It's going to get rough. Stay in town."

"Oh, John, you can be so funny at times. That's one thing I simply love about you." She tried to lean across the table and kiss him again, but he pulled free of her grip and pushed back. Melissa sank back, not the least deterred. "You are right. There's no time to waste."

"Thanks for the meal." It galled him to have a woman pay for him, but she had offered. From what he saw, Rory Randolph made a pile of money from his potboilers, so it wasn't so much Melissa paying as the writer. "You stay here with your boss."

He left, stepping into the wan Idaho sunlight. Turning toward the marshal's office, he plotted and planned how to catch Stringfellow and his gang. The ideas welling up weren't anything the marshal couldn't come up with on his own, but the prisoner might have passed along some better plan.

"Slocum," Marshal Lennox greeted as he pushed into the office. "Set yourself down. I got a bone to pick with you."

Slocum didn't like the sound of that.

"You willing to wait on gettin' your reward for Little Joe?"

"Why?"

"Seems the judge won't pay the money to the blacksmith since he didn't bring in the prisoner. I can pay you and you can pay the smithy."

"That's it?"

Lennox sighed. "I spend more time dealin' with loco mayors and judges than I do catchin' crooks."

"Not much call for that in Idaho Falls."

"It's a peaceable enough town," Lennox admitted. "I reckon you came by with a plan to capture Stringfellow."

"The stagecoach robbery," Slocum said. The marshal nodded.

"That's the way I see it, too. The only time we can know when and where he's goin' to be is that stage."

"His men think they're going to get rich. What's on the stage?"

Lennox rubbed his chin as he thought on this. He studied Slocum closely.

"You dance on both sides of the law, don't you, Slocum?"

"You're working yourself up to asking me for help. Decide for yourself what you want to do. Getting shot at is something I can do on my own."

"Don't doubt that." The marshal took a deep breath and leaned back, laced his fingers behind his head, and went on. "The stagecoach is carrying a gold shipment from mines up in the hills. Most of the mines shut down a while back, but the few that still operate produce enough to make a shipment now and then that's worth the effort to rob."

"As much as six thousand dollars?" Slocum considered how foolish the mine owners were to entrust this much to any stage line. For that much money, a wagon surrounded by a dozen armed guards made more sense.

"Not that. Maybe not even a thousand, but it's still a plum to be picked by the daring. That might be the last gasp from those mines after a new strike farther north in the Bitterroots."

"How many in the posse?"

"I can match Stringfellow's firepower. Four others. Me, you, if you're game."

"Count me in."

"Glad to hear this. You seem like the sort I want at my back. Get your horse and let's ride."

Slocum got to the door when the marshal called after him, "Your twenty-five-dollar reward for Little Joe'll be waitin' when we get back. I promise."

Slocum had to smile at that. Lennox knew the right things to say. Mentioning the money put the notion into a man's head that everyone would come back from successfully catching the Stringfellow gang. Slocum knew better. Any shoot-out, especially with desperados intent on a big robbery, left bodies behind in the dust.

He fetched his horse, mounted, and rode slowly back to the jailhouse. Good as his word, the marshal had four others there ready to ride. Badges gleamed on three of their chests. Seeing that Slocum squinted at the reflections from the badges, Lennox came over and stared up at him.

"I'd give you a deputy's badge, too, but I don't have any more. Fact is, you don't look like the kind who's impressed by what a man wears on his chest."

"Where do we find Stringfellow?"

"Listen up, men," Lennox said loudly, stepping into the center of the posse. "Out at Hangman's Hill, at the summit where a stage team is pulling hard and about exhausted from the steep slope, is where the Stringfellow gang's gonna hold up the stage. We'll stop the robbery, and we'll capture him and the road agents with him. Five dollars a day and a shot of whiskey when we get back."

He went on describing the land. Most of the posse knew the area; Slocum would scout it for himself when he reached the hill.

"You know what to do, men. Let's ride, and let's catch ourselves some desperados."

Lennox swung into the saddle and rode at the head of the posse. Slocum hung back, sizing up the four others. Two had been pulled away from their spot at a saloon and had trouble staying seated. The other two rode side by side and whispered. If they weren't brothers, they were relatives. If one got winged or killed, the other would be worthless for the rest of the fight. Slocum saw that real law enforcement came down to him and the marshal.

He'd started to ride up to speak with the marshal when he heard the thudding of hooves coming up fast behind. Slocum hung back, then forced himself to hold in his anger. Rory Randolph worked to stay in the saddle, but Melissa rode more easily and came even with him. Dust already colored her pale cheeks and turned her into a ghostly creature.

"Go back to town. You and the flimflammer will get hurt or scare off Stringfellow."

"We'll be as quiet as church mice, John. Rory has to see what a real robbery looks like. And how a real hero fights evil. It will make his books ever so much more realistic."

"From what I read in the book about Stringfellow, there's not much real between the covers."

"All the more reason to know how an actual hero like you and Marshal Lennox fight and win. You can't make us go back, John. This is a free country and the road is here for anyone to ride. Please." She began to wheedle when she saw he was adamant about sending her back to Idaho Falls.

"Is he armed?"

"Rory? Why, yes, he has a six-gun."

"Tell him to keep it holstered. Stay back a long way. Otherwise, you're going to be arrested for obstructing justice."

"Thank you, oh, thank you, John!" She leaned over to lightly touch his arm.

He tapped his spurs against the pinto's flanks and rocketed ahead. The road was becoming increasingly hilly, suggesting to Slocum that Hangman's Hill was nearby. He reached Lennox as the marshal slowed and pointed.

"That's the best spot for a road agent," he said. "We'll ride down into the ravine crossing the road, come up, and wait there."

Slocum saw the plan. The stagecoach would struggle to top the hill. That was the best time for Stringfellow and his gang to strike. Lennox intended to come up from downslope and catch the road agents between the stage and drawn six-shooters.

"If Stringfellow gets in front of the stage, he'll be able to escape over the crest."

"With a bigger posse, I'd have men hidin' out on both sides. This is the best we can do with what we got. If I split up so few men, that'll put 'em all at risk."

Before Slocum could argue, the rattle of the coach and the crack of the driver's whip to get the team up the steep slope cut him off. Lennox hastily assembled his small posse. The stage rattled past a hundred yards away and began the hard climb on the hill.

"There they are. Go get 'em, men!" Marshal Lennox shipped out his six-gun and led the charge.

Slocum held back a moment to see if such a frontal assault was the smartest thing to do. He saw only three outlaws coming up behind the stage—but not one of them was Stringfellow. The one named Larry led the other two in firing at the stage. The driver let out a yelp and dropped his whip to use both hands on the reins. With such a slope working against him, he had to keep the team pulling or roll back downhill, dragging the horses.

"Should we join in?"

Slocum saw Rory Randolph waving his six-gun around like a schoolhouse teacher using a pointer.

"Put that away."

"Where is he? Which one's Stringfellow?" Randolph lowered his six-shooter and began firing.

Slocum wheeled about and swatted at the errant marksman. He wanted to drag Randolph from the saddle but only diverted his aim.

"You'll shoot the deputies in the back. Hang back." Slocum put the full bite of command he had learned as an officer during the war into his words. Randolph looked startled and nodded numbly.

That had to be good enough. Slocum knew the marshal needed every gun he could muster. He galloped behind the posse and saw how Lennox was the only one smart enough not to charge up to the outlaws following the road. The deputies didn't realize the danger they faced—until the stagecoach began rolling backward down the hill.

This scattered the posse. One of the gang got caught by the juggernaut thundering backward, but the other two slid to the side of the road and let it pass. The stagecoach tongue had broken and the team reared and dragged the driver from the stage. Slocum saw him hit the ground hard. One hand tangled in the reins. The frightened horses crested the hill, dragging the driver.

Slocum had the chance to join the fight or go after the team and save the driver. He galloped past one outlaw, got off a couple shots that only added to the confusion, and then hit the top of the hill. Stringfellow, Larry, and one other outlaw were just over the crest. He got off a couple more shots. Stringfellow returned them and then Slocum was past and heading downhill after the team. The driver was still caught up in the leather harness.

What saved the driver was the hard pull to the top of the hill. The team had reached a point of exhaustion. Even fear from losing the stage and the loud gunshots couldn't power them past their limits of endurance. Slocum caught up with the lead horse on the right, bent low, and snared the bridle. He reared back. Like a good cow pony, his pinto dug in its hooves and skidded along. The jerk pulled Slocum from the saddle, but it also brought the team to a halt.

He hit the ground hard and came to his feet as quick as a striking snake. Two stumbling steps brought him to the moaning driver. The man's right arm looked a couple inches longer than the left. The reins wrapped around that wrist had cut all the way to the bone. Using his knife, Slocum cut the man free of the leather bonds.

"I'm hurtin' somethin' fierce, mister," the driver said, looking up with haunted eyes. "Help me."

"This is going to hurt a whale of a lot more."

Slocum braced his knee in the man's right armpit, grabbed the injured arm, and yanked hard. He felt the shoulder yield and the arm go back into its socket. The driver passed out from the pain. Having done all he could for the moment, Slocum hauled his Colt back out and looked uphill.

Stringfellow and his men potshot the posse as they tried to come over the top of the hill. Slocum leveled his six-gun and squeezed off a round. Larry threw up his hands, then limply tumbled to the ground. The Colt's hammer fell on a spent cartridge when Slocum tried to repeat the shot with Will Stringfellow in his sights.

Cursing, Slocum worked to knock out the spent brass and reload. He looked back uphill in time to see Rory Randolph come over the top fast and wild. The writer yelled at the top of his lungs and fired his pistol.

A thousand things flashed through Slocum's mind at the same instant. He focused only on Stringfellow, who aimed his six-gun at the writer. Slocum began firing fast. His shots went wild but came close enough to the outlaw leader to spook his horse and ruin any chance he had of shooting Randolph from the saddle.

Then Randolph raced past and cut off any chance Slocum had of hitting the outlaw. More thoughts went through his head. Was it so bad if he shot the writer and then had a clean shot at Stringfellow? But he held up until Randolph bolted downhill away from the road agents. Then he lowered his pistol. The chance to shoot Stringfellow had passed.

The outlaw made an obscene gesture in Randolph's direction, then wheeled about and led his surviving men in retreat as Marshal Lennox and two of the posse rode up, making the countryside sound like Antietam.

Slocum sagged. The chance of killing or capturing Stringfellow had passed. The robbery had been thwarted but at such a cost that the victory might prove worse than letting the road agents steal away the gold.

He knelt and helped the driver sit up. The man's eyelids fluttered as he croaked out, "Damn you."

Slocum wasn't going to argue with him.

7

"It was a mighty good day," Marshal Lennox said. "We lost a couple men, but so did the outlaws."

"The man run over by the stagecoach? How's he doing?" Slocum asked.

"Stove up real bad but the doc says he's gonna make it. But the two road agents you shot . . ." Lennox smiled as he shook his head. "You're a one-man wrecking crew, Slocum. Both of them are ready to be planted in the potter's field."

"Any rewards on their heads?"

"Danged near a hundred dollars." Lennox waited for Slocum to say something more.

When Slocum chewed through it, he finally said, "Give the money to the stage driver. He's going to be out of work for quite a spell."

"The way his arm's all broke up, he'll never drive again."

"I've seen one-armed drivers. If he likes the job, he'll be back at it. Maybe not on that route. Been a while since I saw a grade that steep."

"They do use up teams fast if they have to clear Hangman's Hill." The marshal fell silent, staring hard at Slocum until he worried about what was to come next. The threat of a wanted poster was never more than a heartbeat away with the lawmen who took their jobs the most seriously. Lennox did.

"You want a job, Slocum? I got back the deputy badges I loaned out to the ones in the posse. It can be yours if you want it."

"Me, a deputy? Can't say it's a job I ever sought—"

"Or wanted," Lennox finished for him. "I understand. Remember this, though. Some marshals sportin' badges spent as much time on the other side of the law. That den of thieves down in Abilene and over in Dodge. Don't get me goin' 'bout the ones up here in Idaho and Montana."

"Much obliged for the offer, Marshal, but I've got other fish to fry."

"Better to have the law on your side when you track down Will Stringfellow. Whatever happens then is in the line of duty." He saw the expression on Slocum's face. "Not that it'll matter a whale of a lot to me whether you're wearin' a badge or not when you square off against him."

"I'll let you know, Marshal. Right now, I want to knock back a shot or two and get some rest."

"The others from the posse got their free drinks at the Lucky Seven Saloon. Tell Gustav I sent you."

Slocum took his leave. The weather had turned even colder, the icy wind cutting at his cheeks like invisible razors. He put down his head against the wind and considered his original plan of moving south for the winter. Letting Stringfellow go on his way rankled, but Slocum considered the men he had let off the hook over the years. Too many. They had slipped away more because he had been unable to settle all the scores at once and had to pick and choose where to dispense his own brand of justice.

Letting Stringfellow go now was different. The outlaw had lost some men and either recruited for his gang or lit out for greener pastures, just as Slocum intended when his business here was done.

He went to the saloon and got his drink but saw staying too long wasn't in the cards. The saloon wasn't in a building but a tent that allowed the cold wind to whip under the walls, turning his feet cold as he stood at a plank resting on two shaky sawhorses. The others in the saloon huddled close to a stove at the middle of the tent. None of those who had ridden in the posse were here for Slocum to inquire about what they might have seen. Stringfellow had to be holed up somewhere, and the locals knew every hollow or cave where he might be riding out the weather.

Losing the gold in the shipment had to spark some resentment in the outlaw, too. Slocum tried to understand how Stringfellow would respond. The man was hell-bent for revenge on Rory Randolph and now also needed money to keep going. Asking the marshal about possible shipments might give a hint as to Stringfellow's next move, but with the weather turning colder, the chance of catching him carried added danger. Not only would Slocum have to fight off the outlaws, but he had to deal with storms raging across the Bitterroots.

"Another drink, mister? It's not on the marshal since you was in the posse, but you look like you need it." The barkeep held up a half bottle of whiskey. The amber fluid sloshed about inside, inviting him to sample just another shot.

"Time to grab some shut-eye," Slocum said.

He headed directly for the hotel and got a room. Once inside, he kicked off his boots and stretched out, not bothering to strip off his dusty duds. The bed was as hard as a plank, but Slocum had never felt anything more luxurious under him. In seconds he fell asleep.

He awoke to a frantic banging on the door. He blinked. The room was pitch-dark, and he had pulled his six-shooter out and cocked it without realizing he had done so.

"Who's there?" He leveled the pistol, ready to fire through the door if it became necessary. He was in no mood to fool around.

"John, please. It's me. Melissa. Melissa Benton. You have to let me in."

"Not now." He lay back and closed his eyes. Having her naked body stretched next to him, bare skin against bare skin, would be fine, but not now. Not when he was in such need of sleep.

She kept banging on the door until he considered shooting a round through it to discourage her.

"I need you, John. This is an emergency."

The hysterical note in her voice convinced Slocum he wasn't getting rid of her through persuasion. He got out of bed. The cold floor against his bare feet sent chills all the way up his legs. He shoved his six-shooter back into the holster he still wore and unlocked the door, only to be bowled over as she surged into the room. She threw her arms around him, clinging to him as she buried her face in his shoulder.

Melissa began sobbing. The hot tears soaked into his vest and shirt. He held her awkwardly for a little while longer before peeling her away. Her eyes were bloodshot from crying and she trembled with emotion.

"I need your help, John. Please. Please!"

He kicked the door shut and sat on the bed. She dropped beside him, causing it to cant precariously. Neither noticed.

"He's gone. He's gone!"

"Randolph?"

"He's been kidnapped. It's got to be Stringfellow. There's no other explanation."

"Randolph might be out tomcatting around. Or he could be on a bender. He came within a hair of getting killed out there on the trail. After an experience like that, a man might want to blow off some steam and just give praise for still being on the right side of the dirt."

Slocum had refused to speak to Randolph after his ill-conceived assault. He wasn't able to even aim that hogleg he carried in such a way to threaten the outlaws rather than himself and everyone else in the posse. Randolph's luck had been nothing but good because his horse had tired itself out in a hurry. Otherwise, it would have taken him all the way into the Badlands.

"He wouldn't dare," she said, forcing back tears. A quick dab removed the tears welling in her eyes. "He's been kidnapped. I know it."

"Go to the marshal. He's the law in town."

"You're responsible for him, John. You're our guide."

Slocum's sleepiness burned off. He had never agreed to work for the writer. After what happened to Merriman and how determined Stringfellow was to ventilate the writer, he wasn't sure anyone with a brain in their head would take the job.

"What do you want me to do?"

"Find him. Get him back safely. It's important. He . . . he can't die."

"When was the last time you saw him?"

"Just before he went to his room. We had eaten dinner. He was tired, and I wanted to return to my room to do some writing. To make notes about all that'd happened today."

"He's not there?"

"I knocked. He didn't answer. It's not like Rory."

Slocum thought the writer had probably found a bottle and had passed out in his room. He found his boots and pulled them on. Then he made sure his six-shooter rode easy on his hip. He stood and held out his hand to get Melissa off the bed.

"Show me his room."

"Oh, John, thank you." She tried to hug him, but he held her at bay. He wanted to sleep, and the sooner he found Randolph for her, the sooner he could get back to bed.

She led him to the lobby, clinging to his hand. The clerk sat in a chair behind the desk, feet hiked to the counter and head rocked back. He snored loud enough to drown out a sawmill. Melissa tugged insistently on Slocum's hand and they went up the steep, narrow stairs. In the hallway she stopped in front of the first door.

"Go on, knock."

Slocum was in no mood to repeat what the woman claimed to have done. He reared back and kicked out like a mule. The lock broke and the door slammed hard against the inner wall. Slocum blocked its return with his elbow as he bulled his way into the room. An oil lamp had been lit and turned low, giving him plenty of light to see what he had gotten himself into.

Shreds of paper littered the room, as if a snowstorm had blown through. Slocum shivered because the window was thrown wide and cold wind blew into his face.

"What happened to him? How'd this happen?" Melissa moaned behind him as she peered over his shoulder.

Slocum opened the wardrobe. Randolph's flashy duds still hung there. Whatever Randolph had been wearing was all he had hanging on his back.

"His gun's gone," Slocum said, rummaging through the writer's belongings. "Was he wearing a holster when you left him?"

"He was, I think. Yes, he had the gun strapped to his hip."

"Did you hear any shots?"

"No. I kept knocking but no response, and the door was locked." Melissa looked at the splintered door where Slocum had kicked it open. "I'll have to pay for the damage."

Slocum picked up a piece of the paper and held it so he could read. One of Randolph's books had been ripped apart. Slocum couldn't tell if it was a duplicate copy of the one he still had in his pocket. He held out a large piece to the woman.

"Which book is this?"

She examined it, then looked up. Her face turned even paler than it had been before. She opened her mouth to speak, then clamped her lips shut. She turned from him as she began sobbing.

"It's the new book. Another one with Stringfellow as the villain."

"Worse than the other?"

"Oh, yes, far worse. In this one, Stringfellow is a *villain*."

Considering how the other book had begun, Slocum tried to imagine how this was possible and failed.

"Could Stringfellow have bought a copy of this?"

"I suppose. How the books make it across the country is something of a mystery, but they do. Some go around the Horn or across the Panamanian Isthmus to San Francisco. Out here, the books are shipped up the Missouri or as freight in a train, from Chicago or Saint Louis."

"This might have caused Stringfellow to come after your boss, as if he hadn't before."

"We should never have come to the West," she cried.

Slocum didn't try comforting her. He went to the window and looked out. The wooden ledge was nicked from a recent scuffle as if someone with spurs had entered and left this way. From other evidence someone had been dragged through the window. Slocum leaned far out and tried to make out the ground below. No light came from windows beneath this room, keeping him from seeing what was there.

He pushed past Melissa and went down the stairs to the lobby, where the clerk still sawed wood. The man stirred a little as Slocum opened the door and let in a cold draft but didn't awaken until Melissa rushed after him, crying out for him to help Randolph. Slocum ignored her and went around the hotel to a spot under the second-story window. He walked around, saw the hoofprints and where two pairs of boots had left deep impressions. The tracks led out of town toward the distant mountains.

"What happened, John? He's been kidnapped, hasn't he?"

"Come along," he said. When she hesitated, he grabbed her hand and pulled her behind him. "We're going to let the marshal know what's happened."

"I don't trust him," she said. "I trust you, John. You'll do the right thing."

"That's what I intend doing," he said.

Slocum had to pull Melissa the entire way to the

jailhouse. He opened the door and shoved her inside ahead of him. Marshal Lennox jerked awake. He had been sleeping, his head on his crossed arms on the desk.

"What's wrong?" The marshal rubbed his eyes and coughed. This seemed to be all it took to get him fully awake.

"The writer fellow's been kidnapped, probably by Will Stringfellow." Slocum shoved Melissa toward the chair so she'd sit. "Miss Benton saw he was gone and asked me to be sure."

"You workin' for Randolph now?" The marshal took a deep breath and looked disapproving. After all, he had offered Slocum what he considered to be a better job as deputy.

"Nope, I was just handy." Slocum related what he had found. "If you send out a posse, you can run them to ground after sunup."

"A posse? Why'd I send out a posse when there's no proof Stringfellow has anything to do with this? Hell, there's not even proof any crime's been committed. Writers are peculiar fellows. He might have just upped and took off on his own."

"After tearing up a book critical of Stringfellow? By going out the window?"

"As I said, writers are peculiar characters. I met Mark Twain once, down in Virginia City, but that wasn't even his real name. Clemens or something like it was. He said it a nom de plume. The only folks who go by nom de plumes are crooks."

"Or writers," Slocum added. Lennox nodded in agreement.

"What's wrong with you? Rory's gone! Tell him, John. You said you found two sets of tracks. Who else but Stringfellow would ride off with Randolph?"

"Now, Miss Benton, that's a question only you can answer. You and him, are you . . . ?" Lennox let the sentence trail off as he primed the pump for a sexy revelation.

"Are you asking if Rory and I are lovers? I should say not! He's my—" She cut off her words, swallowed hard, and took a deep breath after she composed herself. "He's my employer and nothing more."

Slocum had heard lies in his day. This was a whopper. He tried to imagine the lovely woman naked alongside Randolph in bed. It was just as well that he couldn't, but why else would a man bring such a lovely woman out West with him? She took notes, but as far as he could tell, Melissa did nothing else for Randolph. So why did he think she was lying?

"I'm the town marshal, and my jurisdiction doesn't extend outside of Idaho Falls. There's no reason—or legal justification—for me to go traipsin' off to find Randolph. I'd have to leave the town without a lawman since I don't have a full-time deputy." Lennox fixed Slocum with his cold, accusing gaze.

Slocum felt no guilt at not agreeing to be the man's deputy. He wasn't cut out to be a lawman, here or anywhere else.

"But you went after Stringfellow when he tried to rob the stagecoach! That was outside town!"

"I had firsthand information Stringfellow was going to rob the stage. Nothing in what you or Slocum says gives me any proof of a crime."

"But Rory—"

"Might have upped and run off with a lover," Lennox said. "You claimed you and him weren't in any kind of relationship like that. Might be he found a local gal, they hit it off, and him and her's off for a tryst." Lennox smiled. "That's a word I came across in a Brit book. Tryst. It means—"

"I know what it means, dammit," raged Melissa. "I'm a writer. You have to save Rory from Stringfellow."

Lennox shook his head. "Sorry, Miss Benton. It's out of my hands. The good citizens of Idaho Falls wouldn't want me leavin' on what's likely a wild-goose chase. If you think Randolph's in big trouble, Sheriff Mueller's got jurisdiction in all of Bonneville County."

"Where can I find the sheriff?" Melissa sat with her arms crossed over her chest, glaring at the marshal.

"I can't rightly say. He was down along the Snake River hunting for a prison escapee last I heard. That was a week back. Maybe two."

"So you won't help." Melissa turned to Slocum and looked at him imploringly. "Please, John. Bring Rory back."

"I've got other things to occupy me," he said. "Good night, Marshal, Miss Benton." With that, he left the sputtering woman in the jailhouse. He figured the marshal was used to handling angry women. If he wasn't, he was a quick study and would learn fast.

8

Slocum couldn't get warm enough. He needed a new winter coat to wear beneath his duster. Even wearing the canvas duster in the saloon—this one had solid wood walls—he was cold. The crafty wind snaked through the cracks in the wood, through unsealed knotholes, and even up from under the floorboards to bite him with cold fangs.

"Another shot," he said.

Money running low, Slocum carefully spread the greenbacks out on the bar, counting them carefully. The marshal had squeezed the reward for the two outlaws he had killed from the judge and had given it over to the injured stagecoach driver. The earlier reward for Little Joe had been spent, paid to the blacksmith. He now had two horses, although the pinto was sturdy enough for anything he'd want. Finding anyone interested in buying the jailed outlaw's horse had proven difficult because they worried about retribution from Stringfellow or the others in his gang.

Taking the horse to Pocatello or even farther south and selling it required time and effort. Slocum hadn't decided whether to keep it and make the trip to El Paso faster than he could have on one horse. Riding until the pinto tired, then switching to the outlaw's horse while the pinto rested, added miles to a day's travel. With the teeth of Idaho winter sharpening daily, he had to leave soon.

"There you are."

Slocum glanced over his shoulder to see Marshal Lennox push through the door, then fight it closed against the wind. The lawman came over and leaned on the bar next to him.

"A beer, Sally."

The tired woman in the canvas apron behind the bar gave him a weak smile, drew the beer, and slid it in front of the marshal. He dropped a dime on the bar. She didn't bother making change for the nickel beer. Slocum got the feeling more went on between the marshal and the barkeep than simply serving him his liquor.

"I'm still not interested," Slocum said by way of preamble. "Fact is, I'm thinking on what supplies I'll need so I can leave before the snows come."

"That might be outside a week. I've got a gimpy knee, but it's not hurtin' me much yet. No storm, not for a week."

"Good," Slocum said. Inside he tensed as the marshal sipped on his brew. The man was too calm and composed.

"She's gone."

"What?" Slocum looked hard at the lawman. "What are you talking about?"

"Your lady friend. The one who works for the writer fellow. Gutherie over at the hotel said she left early this morning, before sunup. He tried to find out where she was going, but she wouldn't answer him."

Slocum knocked back his shot. The whiskey burned all the way down but gave him no soothing puddle of warmth in his belly. Instead, it churned as if it might burn through the bottom of his stomach and drip out with his guts onto the saloon floorboards.

"Gutherie said she was dressed for travel. For the trail. He thinks she lit out after Randolph."

"She doesn't know squat about tracking."

"That's less a worry than not knowing how to survive out in the mountains with the weather turning brisk."

"Brisk?" Slocum laughed without humor at that. He shivered every time a new gust of wind rattled the walls and shook the door. "I surely don't want to be here when you get around to calling it cold."

"That won't be for another month. There has to be more than two feet of snow on the ground for local folks to say it's cold."

Slocum silently passed over one of the greenbacks and exchanged it for a full bottle of whiskey. Sally never said a word. She seemed to know instinctively what he wanted. He poured himself a single shot, then made certain the cork securely stoppered the contents.

"She went north. Are you headin' in that direction, too?"

Slocum hefted the bottle, looked at the marshal, and said, "Go to hell."

Lennox laughed at him the entire way out of the saloon and into the fierce wind.

Following Melissa's trail proved easy enough. She made no effort to hide it. The wind blew dead leaves and dust over the trail, but much of her trail had been laid down in mud. The wind dried out the mud quickly and turned it to crumbling dirt, but that retained the imprint as if chiseled into the ground. What worried Slocum more than the cold was the woman actually finding Stringfellow. The outlaw wouldn't treat her kindly.

Why he had kidnapped Randolph was obvious enough. A clever man might torture another for days or even weeks. In this weather, the ways of inflicting pain increased. Heat followed by cold. Tiny cuts that oozed until the blood froze, sealing the wounds. Slocum had even heard stories of using icicles as a means of torture. They pierced the skin easily, then melted, spreading cold from the inside out. That very cold served to deaden pain and give further opportunities for torture.

If Stringfellow was royally pissed at the publication of a second book detailing his shortcomings as a human being, he might keep Randolph alive most of the winter until the man went crazy.

Slocum had to think Rory Randolph wasn't far from being loco at the best of times. He obviously thought he knew how to ride and shoot like the cowboys and lawmen and villains he wrote about. The sight of him coming over Hangman's Hill, firing wildly as he fought to stay astride his runaway horse, put the lie to any expertise. Coming out to Stringfellow's stomping grounds in answer to the outlaw's challenge had to be stupider than crazy, Slocum decided. Randolph thought too much of his own abilities. Or maybe he no longer separated the fiction he wrote from the harsh reality of the world.

Slocum pulled his duster closer around him. He hadn't bought a heavy coat but had dickered for a lighter one he could afford. He wore his longjohns, shirt, vest, coat, and duster and still the wind sneaked in to torment him. Long since, he had lost feeling in his toes. He paused to look up into a U-shaped pass where Melissa had already ridden. He was used to such punishment and cold weather. She was a hothouse flower in comparison. She might be determined, and he had seen an iron core to her that would prevent her from ever giving up on her boss, but years of easy living would trump all that.

High society in New York City never exposed her to the elements blowing off the mountains right now. And the wind and weather only got worse as the season crept on.

He pulled up his bandanna over his nose and mouth and lowered his head so the brunt of the wind struck the brim of his Stetson. Tracking Melissa was easy, but he saw nothing of the trail she followed. How had she decided this was the way to go to rescue Randolph? If the writer had been taken from his room when she said, the trail would be hours old. She wouldn't be able to keep Stringfellow and her boss in sight to steer herself that way.

Slocum got a little colder at the idea that Stringfellow lured her on. He might have purposefully ridden slowly, waiting to see if she would come after him. He lured her deeper into the mountains as part of his revenge against Randolph.

As Slocum reached the broad saddle of the pass, he discarded that notion. Stringfellow didn't have even a hint of subtlety in him. Why lead her on when he could just get the drop on her, hog-tie her, or otherwise capture her and spirit her off with Randolph?

Standing in the stirrups, he turned watering eyes down the far side of the pass. The terrain leveled out into a meadow now gone brown with winter. What greenery remained were the junipers and pines sprouting up in tight knots as far as he could see. He lifted his eyes to the tree line a couple thousand feet above. Dabs of snow on the bare rock there hinted at worse weather to come. Soon. He put no store in Lennox's knee or the idea that a storm might be a week off. From the clouds slipping and sliding past the highest peaks, a storm might come lashing down on him at any time.

On him and Melissa.

Stringfellow had been raiding for some time to know the country well and would survive. What he did with Randolph was more simple retribution than murder, the way Slocum saw it. If Randolph had written about him what he had about Will Stringfellow, his head would have been stuck on a spear somewhere near town so everyone could see it and learn not to bad-mouth any man like he had in *Backshooting Badman of the Badlands*.

Slocum took advantage of a momentary lull in the wind to speed down into the meadow. Melissa's trail became muddled there, and it took him some time to find it again. Twenty minutes on the trail brought him up short. He cursed himself for being a fool and worse. He had committed a simple mistake that might cause the woman's death. He kicked his leg over the back of the horse and dismounted.

On his knees, he brushed away leaves and got down low to let the setting sun catch the edges of the hoofprint in the dirt. Gently moving away debris from the best of the prints, he pushed his face down close, then sat back and shook his head.

"An Indian pony," he said softly. The words became garbled in the rising wind. He checked once more to assure himself he wasn't wrong now, then stood. "Damnation. She's got a brave on her trail."

He swung into the saddle and rode faster now. Melissa had to know where she rode. There hadn't been the slightest deviation in her course from Idaho Falls. How she knew where Stringfellow had taken Randolph was something of a poser, but Slocum couldn't rule out the possibility that the outlaw had given her a map to egg her on. Still, even if Stringfellow had let her know where he'd made his camp, the woman rode with single-minded determination. No side trips, no missed turns anywhere along the way. She had ridden straight for the saddle pass and once through it hadn't spent any time hunting for the right trail.

Where she had picked up the Indian trailing her was something Slocum couldn't answer. There had been only one trail through the pass. The brave had come across her after she reached the meadow, or he might have thought she'd hired him to guide her. That explained how she had ridden straight as an arrow for this section of the mountains, but evidence on the ground showed the Indian rode a considerable distance behind her. Perhaps even an hour behind, which meant Slocum would overtake the brave before he found Melissa.

An Indian scout didn't mean anything in particular. Slocum had not heard of any tribe on the warpath. This time of year, a solitary rider usually turned out to be a hunter or a scout for a larger band as they migrated out of the higher pastures in search of better weather and less snow.

Still, Slocum hadn't paid a powerful lot of attention to what the various tribes were up to. A fight between clans could boil over into deadly warfare. The cavalry might have taken it into its collective head to run the Blackfoot out of the territory. That had happened before, to deadly effect for the better part of a summer. He had missed the worst of the fighting since he had ridden farther north from the Oregon coast hunting for work. The Appaloosa ranch to the west had gone belly up when the owner couldn't keep his gambling under control. The Blackfoot fight had only added to Slocum's wariness back then before he got the job where he'd spent last summer.

Most of the tribes were content to live and let live, although the declining numbers of buffalo gave most of them trouble feeding their clans. An especially cold winter would bring starvation to some of the Indians, but Slocum saw no reason for them to go on the warpath now. Stealing, raids, those were acts of desperation after the food began to run low.

He entered the woods at the far side of the mountain pasture. The darkness wrapped him like a shroud. The chill wind slashed at him and made riding even more of a chore. By the time he blundered through in almost total darkness, he wondered why he bothered with Melissa at all. He had nothing but contempt for her employer. The brief tryst with her by the watering pond had been enjoyable enough, but she had done nothing but bring him trouble since.

The word "tryst" buzzed in his head. He remembered the marshal using it and feeling proud at his book learning. He also remembered how irate Melissa had become at the suggestion she and Randolph were more than employer and employee. Slocum wondered what the truth was. If she wasn't his lover, she showed devotion to him far beyond what anyone expected of a paid servant.

He left the woods and found himself bathed in the silver light of a half-moon poking above the distant mountain peaks. Slocum slowed and tried to find the trail again. He might have lost both Melissa and the Indian in the woods. As he tried to find any spoor, he heard a loud neighing from his left. He turned, cocked his head, and listened hard. More noise drew him like a magnet.

He pushed aside his duster and fumbled under the thin coat to find the butt of his Colt. Fighting an Indian in the dark struck him as chancy. Better to sneak up and shoot the man in the back than risk a long fight where the Indian had all the advantages. Slocum was no tenderfoot, but he also hadn't spent his entire life living in the woods and depending on every meal being brought in by his own skill and wit. Spending the summer with a crew herding cattle was hard work, but the food at the end of the day was supplied. He didn't have to keep the beeves together, then go hunt for whatever he ate.

This was the first time Slocum had thought of being a wrangler as easy work. Compared to living in the woods and not knowing where the next meal came from, it was.

What was Melissa experiencing?

He rode toward the sounds of the horse, then slowed when the noises stopped. He tried to make out what lay ahead, but trees dotted the terrain again. As bright as the moon was, he couldn't make out anyone in front of him. As that thought hit him, Slocum doubled back to be sure he hadn't picked up someone after him. Because he had found traces of one kind didn't mean there weren't two—or more.

A ten-minute hunt revealed nothing. He felt a little better about pushing ahead past where he had hesitated before. He saw evidence in a drifted pile of snow with an icy crust where another horse had passed. The edges were sharp and hadn't spent a moment's time in the sun. The sound of a horse pushing through undergrowth spurred him on. Less worried about falling into a trap himself, Slocum rode to rescue Melissa from whatever trouble she had gotten herself into.

He came out in another clearing. She stood beside her

horse on the far side, fiddling with the bridle and paying no attention to anything around her. Slocum scanned the area and immediately spotted the Indian brave coming from the shadows. Like the woman, he paid no heed to the world around. He was intent on creeping up on Melissa and nothing else.

Whatever he wanted of her, he wasn't being open about it. To Slocum's mind that meant the brave wanted to take her as either a squaw or a slave. Neither would suit the citified Melissa Benton.

The Indian slid from horseback and moved like a ghost toward the unsuspecting woman.

9

Slocum put his head down and spurred his pinto to full speed. The sound of pounding hooves against the frozen ground warned the brave that his attack wasn't going as smoothly as he had expected. He spun about and drew his knife. The flash of silver in the moonlight warned Slocum he might end up dead if he didn't play his cards right. He should have drawn and fired as fast as he could at the brave, but he worried there might be others nearby. The gunshots might draw them. If he killed the Indian, Slocum might never find out why he was roaming about the mountains in the dead of night.

Slocum kicked free of the stirrups and launched himself. He collided with the brave, his shoulder crushing into the man's chest. The impact knocked the knife from the Indian's hand, but it took nothing else from his fight. A strong hand grabbed the back of Slocum's neck and squeezed hard. Lightning pain filled his head. He kicked hard, found something softer than the ground, and kicked again. His knee smashed into the man's groin. The Indian grunted. His grip lessened on Slocum's neck, letting him roll to his feet. The two men squared off against each other, masked by night.

As they circled, Slocum caught a glimpse of his opponent's face. No war paint. The Indians weren't on the warpath. That meant a solitary hunter or scout. That emboldened Slocum. He charged, got his arms wrapped around a taut waist, and then he heaved. Fingers laced at the small of the Indian's back, Slocum lifted upward, twisted, and slammed him to the ground. The impact knocked the wind from the scout's lungs.

Slocum scrambled to get to his feet and draw his six-shooter. He pointed it at the Indian and demanded, "Where's your camp? How many are there?"

"John, be careful!"

Distracted, Slocum looked toward Melissa. This gave his captive time to kick out. A moccasin-clad foot struck his wrist and sent his six-gun flying into the darkness. Rather than pursue the fight, the Indian rolled, climbed up on a stump, and jumped, landing hard astride his pony. The horse galloped off into the night.

"Stop him, John. Who is that? He must know where Rory is!"

Slocum paid her no attention as he hunted for his six-shooter. He found the Colt in a pile of dried pine needles. After brushing off the sticky needles, he thrust the gun back into his cross-draw holster. Only then did he go to Melissa's side.

"What the hell are you doing?" He hardly contained his anger. "You could have been killed. That was an Indian. A Cree, by the way he was dressed."

"So?"

"They go by another name. Cree is their name for themselves. Settlers in these parts call them the Blood Indians. They were run out of Canada and don't have much liking for the white man."

"Why don't they go back to Canada then?"

"Because the Canadian government wanted their land and took it. Their marshals, the North West Mounted Rifles, chased the Indians south."

"I have never heard of them."

"They changed their name a couple years back to the North-West Mounted Police. Same former army officers, same government policy. It's been a bone of contention about letting the Cree stay here, but to send them north means they'd be exterminated."

"How terrible," she said, but her tone carried no concern. "Would that red man have scalped me?"

"Not likely. He'd have taken you as a slave, and all the braves in his tribe would have used you."

"Used me? What do you mean? Oh," she said, her hand going to her mouth. "That's barbaric. Do all the Indians do that?"

Before he could answer, she fumbled out a pad of paper and a pencil and scribbled away. She looked up, her pale face turned to flashing silver in the moonlight.

"I need to make a note of this before the details fade."

"Why?"

"Because it makes for fascinating detail in a story. I—Rory, that is—will find the exact place to work it into the next novel. That's why we came out here to the frontier, after all."

"You came out because of Will Stringfellow," he said. "You had a death wish and wanted to see what the man you bad-mouthed was like. You never thought he would be mad at what Randolph wrote. You thought he would be happy to be notorious."

"You can't claim that we slandered him. No, I think the proper term is *libel*," she said. She wet the tip of the pencil and scratched out a few more lines before putting the pad and pencil into her coat pocket.

"Why'd you leave town? You couldn't be stupid enough to think you would find your boss."

"Neither you nor that lickspittle marshal could bestir your bones to rescue Rory. I had to do so."

"Why risk your life like this?"

"I . . . I need him," she said.

"You need him like a bull needs teats. I tracked you. You never veered from a route straight here. Did Stringfellow leave you a map? Somehow entice you to come out?"

"He knows nothing of my rescue attempt," she said. "As to how I knew where to go, well, it was obvious that the outlaw had read Rory's novel about him."

"So what?"

"The outlaw gang's hideout is exactly located in the book. We are within a few miles of it." She turned around, got her bearings, and then pointed toward the highest peaks in the distant mountains. "That way."

Slocum stared at her as if she had turned plumb loco.

"Why do you think Stringfellow used a spot you mentioned in a book as his hideout?"

"Because it is the best possible location for any road agent on the run."

"How do you know?"

She stepped closer and looked up at him. He read the scorn on her face but refused to back down. With her index finger, she stabbed down into his chest.

"Research, that's why I know things like that. I pored over government maps of the region showing topography for more than a week. Rory's books are nothing if not accurate."

"Calling Stringfellow a sister-raper and a mother-killer sounds real accurate."

"Oh, that was literary license. Characters aren't meant to be real. But the background has to be. The readers demand it."

Slocum said nothing about the one reader who wanted to lift Rory Randolph's scalp. Even if Melissa was right about Stringfellow using the same hideout as mentioned in the book, nothing said that the author was still among the living.

The only thing that made Slocum think the writer was alive was not finding his corpse on the ride into the mountains. Stringfellow had no reason to give a proper burial to a man who had lied so outrageously about him and then published it for the world to see.

"I don't want to camp the night. Is your horse up to the trip back to town?"

"I should say not," Melissa cried, stamping her foot. "That is, the horse is able to go the distance, but I am not returning until I have rescued Rory."

Slocum considered tying her up and dragging her back that way. He wasn't sure what the marshal would do to him for kidnapping her. Probably nothing, but that didn't solve any problem. The instant he turned his back, she would return to free her boss. Telling her he would press on and save Randolph solved nothing either. She wouldn't believe him. Keeping an eye out for how she might get him killed as she tried sneaking about was worse than agreeing to ride with her to the supposed outlaw camp.

The notion that Stringfellow actually used the novel as a map for his hideout struck him as about the most preposterous thing in the world. Then he realized nothing about the writer and his secretary had been ordinary. If he had a lick of sense, he would ride in the opposite direction Melissa took and never stop until the sun burned his face, tequila rolled down his gullet, and lovely señoritas fawned over him.

If he did that, he would eventually hear how he had been written into one of Randolph's books as a treacherous back-stabbing son of a bitch. Considering what he had written about a man he knew only from a wanted poster, that might be mild. Slocum hated the idea of tracking the writer down and putting a bullet in his head. From all he had heard, the New York City Police weren't inclined to believe he would be justified.

"It's too dark to ride without getting into trouble," he told her. "We can camp here and start at first light."

"Rory needs rescuing."

"He's dead by now," Slocum said harshly. "If I rode in Stringfellow's gang, I'd kill him if Stringfellow wouldn't. There's no reason to kidnap him and not kill him."

"He was mighty foolish to tear up the book like that. Why, it had some chapters in it that made Stringfellow out to be almost . . . noble. Almost."

"The best we're going to do is make Stringfellow show us the body."

"No, we press on. Now. Will you help me up, John?"

He snorted. His breath came out in twin gusts like smoke from a dragon's snout. He whistled and got his pinto trotting over. Let Melissa go on any way she could. He stepped up to see her climb onto a lightning-struck stump, then almost gingerly take her seat. The ride had worn her fine backside raw. Slocum found himself remembering how he had stroked over that bottom, then unblistered.

"Well?"

Slocum jerked around. She had been speaking, and he had missed everything, lost in memory of a far more delightful moment with her.

"What's your plan?" she asked. "How do you intend to free Rory?"

"That depends on if he's still alive. If he is, how does Stringfellow have him tied up? There's no reason to make plans that have to be changed because I had no idea about the actual lay of the land."

"There is an overhang. The outlaws will pitch their tents there."

"Tents?"

"Perhaps they don't have tents. All right, that is where they will unroll their blankets. If they are smart, they will put their horses in a corral not far downslope near a stream. Any prisoner will be kept between the horses and where they sleep."

Slocum let her rattle on about how to approach the camp.

It meant nothing until he saw what was possible. He doubted Stringfellow had the writer in camp or anywhere. A captive made future robberies difficult, especially since Slocum had put two of the gang into graves. Putting Rory under guard kept one outlaw from serious robbing. A dead body merely drew flies.

"Hold up," Slocum said. He bent over and grabbed Melissa's reins when she didn't stop. "We're riding into a trap."

"How can you tell?"

The foot-long orange-yellow muzzle flash dazzled Slocum. He jerked hard on the captive reins and caused Melissa's horse to rear, throwing her to the ground. He dropped the reins when she was safely out of the line of fire, flopping around on the ground like a fish out of water, and went for his six-shooter. He bent low and kicked at his horse's flanks to mount a full frontal assault. By the time he had narrowed the distance to a dozen yards, he started firing.

A second shot rang out. He adjusted his aim and sighted in on a spot just under the muzzle. He heard a loud groan that made his hope spiral upward. He doubted he had killed their ambusher, but he had winged him. Bad, from the sound of the groaning.

Hooves pounded as the sniper tried to ride off. Slocum shoved his pistol back into his holster and concentrated on riding through the low-hanging branches and thickets. He burst out into a clearing to see the Indian clinging to his horse's neck. Before they vanished into another copse, the Indian fell from his mount and bounced along on the ground to lie still.

Slocum kept riding, captured the runaway horse, and then returned. The Indian stirred but wasn't moving in any way threatening.

"You shot?"

He hadn't expected an answer and wasn't surprised. With a quick move, he dropped to the ground and went to the fallen man. The blood on his chest looked like a pool of pitch in the moonlight. Slocum stripped back the buckskin and examined the wound.

"Slug's still in your shoulder. Bite down on this." Slocum moved the man's arm up over his mouth so a piece of buckskin dangled down. The Indian did as he was told. Slocum took out his knife, knelt so his knee pressed firmly into the man's chest to keep him from floundering about, then began digging. Before the slug popped free, the brave had passed out.

Slocum stood and looked down at the man.

"You killed him?"

"Come on over," Slocum called to Melissa. She had stopped a dozen yards away. "I need help with him."

She dismounted and walked closer, her horse trailing behind.

"You knocked me off, and I hurt myself."

"It got you out of the line of fire. You would have ended up like him if I hadn't."

"You shot him?"

"Just plucked this out of his hide." He took her hand, dropped the bloody bullet into it, then closed it. "Keep it as research material."

He was startled when she opened her fist and examined it carefully under the moonlight.

"It is hardly deformed."

"What's scraped off it was done by my knife as I dug around. He would have got blood poisoning if I hadn't cut it out."

"What are you going to do with him? We have to press on and rescue Rory."

"We can do that, but then he'll die."

"He's a savage. He tried to murder us. Me. Leave him."

"In this weather, he'll be dead before morning. You want a man's life on your hands?"

"Of course not, but he tried to murder me. Us. He's not a friend."

"But he is a human being," Slocum said. He knelt and rolled the man over so he could get his arms around him. He heaved the Indian to his feet, then lifted and draped him over his horse. "I've got to tie him down."

"A good idea. Hold him prisoner and you can turn him over to the marshal when we return to town."

"Nope, got a better idea what to do with him."

"But you said you weren't going to abandon him to the elements."

"I'm taking him back to his tribe. They can't be camped too far from here."

"John, no!"

He used some rope from his lariat to lash the Indian onto his horse so he wouldn't slide off. Then he closed his eyes, tilted his head back, and took a deep whiff. Wood smoke from a cooking fire not a mile upwind reached him. From the scent he knew no white man fixed that meal. It had to be where the brave had ridden from.

Walking, he led his and the Indian's horses behind him. Melissa shouted and carried on, calling him names he had never heard in all his born days, but she eventually fell into step beside him. He guessed she was grateful for the chance to walk and not ride, but from all the venom she spewed, it was hard to say she would ever be happy about anything ever again.

10

"I'll leave and find Rory on my own. I was doing just fine until you came along."

Slocum glanced at Melissa. She rode with her back rigid and eyes straight ahead. He couldn't tell in the dark but thought her hands shook to match the tremor in her voice. She was either angry or scared.

"Getting the brave back to his people matters more right now."

"You think Stringfellow killed Rory. I don't."

"You have some evidence on your side," Slocum admitted. "If Stringfellow wanted him dead, he could have killed him in the hotel instead of carting him away."

"See? You agree with me."

"No, I'm thinking Stringfellow kidnapped him to torture him at his leisure, to not worry about people in the other rooms complaining about Randolph screaming as his skin was flayed off."

"You're terrible. Despicable. Horrible."

"Others might say I'm being realistic," Slocum said. He

let the Indian pony have its head. He had a good idea where the Cree camp was from the cooking odors and wood smoke, but the pony proved a better guide when they reached a swiftly flowing river.

Fording it in the dark was a sure way of dying. The horse avoided what might have been the spot Slocum would have chosen and trotted upriver a quarter mile. From what he could tell from the smoke and sounds carrying downwind and over the rush of the river, they rode away from the camp. But the horse found a spot where it stood and stared at the far side of the river.

"We cross here," Slocum said.

"But there's no way to know how deep it is. We might be swept away. The current is quite strong."

"It is," Slocum said. "And returning the brave to his tribe might speed up the hunt for Stringfellow and your boss."

"Do you think they've seen Stringfellow?"

"If the Cree have camped here very long, they've seen him. They don't miss anything."

"Why wouldn't they attack him?"

"His gang might stop them. Or Stringfellow doesn't have anything they want. This isn't a raiding party. The scout was on the lookout for food. They want to lay in as much as they can before winter hits hard."

Even as he spoke, a cold wind ripped at his face and hands. Getting soaked in the river would make it even worse. With the temperature dropping, ice might freeze on their clothing. Slocum realized the gamble he took returning the Indian to his tribe. They had to be grateful, take in a white man and woman, and eventually part with information about white outlaws. That was a powerful lot of trust on the Indians' part when it had been Slocum who had shot the brave because the brave was shooting at him.

"Should we wait until we can see? This crossing looks very dangerous." Melissa pushed back her hair, so black it disappeared into the night and left only her pale face lit by the moon as if it were a silver-white mask. He saw the concern.

He almost laughed at her. She had come out on her own, sure she knew where Randolph was hidden away. How she figured to rescue him was something Slocum had never gotten clear in his head. Now she worried about crossing a river in the dark. Just because an Indian pony stopped and looked across.

Slocum realized how much trust he placed in that horse. He grabbed the reins, tugged, and got the horse moving. He kept pace beside it with his pinto picking out a way on the slippery rocks just under the inky surface. As the water rose to the horses' bellies, Slocum worried the Indian might drown. He urged the horses to greater speed and soon reached the far side, dripping wet, cold, but safe.

He looked back across the river where Melissa sat astride her nervous horse, watching intently.

"I think I see where the bottom is," she said. She looked up anxiously. "This is going to be a grand adventure, whatever happens." She put her heels to the horse's flanks and got it walking into the rushing river.

Slocum watched for any sign of her being swept away. If the current pulled her from the saddle, he had only a few seconds to save her before she vanished through the churning, white-capped rapids and into the night. Her crossing was less sure than Slocum's, but she finally reached the shore beside him.

Her teeth chattered loudly as she tried to speak.

"The Cree will have fires for us to dry our clothes," he said.

"I h-h-hope so. I'll catch my death of cold if I don't get dry soon."

Slocum bent low and checked to be sure the brave hadn't drowned when he wasn't looking. The man stirred and raised his head a little.

"You'll be back with your tribe in a few minutes,"

Slocum assured him. He received a skeptical look, then a tiny smile before the Cree sank back.

"Come on," Slocum said.

He didn't have to tell Melissa to keep up. She shivered and cursed and made squishy sounds as she rode, her skirts heavy with water. For his own part, water had seeped over the tops of his boots. If he tried to walk, the sucking noise would be louder than if he whooped and hollered. Realizing this, he made no effort to approach the Cree camp quietly.

Two sentinels popped up when he rode forward. They lifted their rifles and started to fire. Slocum quickly signed to them he had one of their tribe with him. As one guard kept him covered, the other raised the brave's head so he could see who Slocum had brought back. A rapid exchange between the guards sent the one who had been covering them racing off to a tipi near the center bonfire. A tall man who moved slowly and carefully from old age came out.

"You bring back my brother's son."

"He's been shot. You need to get your medicine man working on him. I dug out the bullet, but he's still weak."

The Indian whom Slocum took to be the chief motioned. Half the camp had come to see what the nocturnal disturbance was all about. The injured brave was pulled from horseback and carried away.

"What do we do now, John?" Melissa rode close. Her wet skirt pressed into his equally wet jeans-clad leg.

"Wait and see what happens."

He sat easily, outwardly calm, but inside his gut churned. A dozen braves circled them now. The time for stealth or fighting had passed. Only diplomacy won them their freedom— and lives.

"They don't look friendly."

"They don't look unfriendly," Slocum countered.

They were in a staring match, neither side saying anything. Slocum kept motioning Melissa to silence. Seconds dragged into long minutes until the chief spoke.

"I know you."

"I know you also, wise chief. You were gracious and accepted my chief's gift of food."

"Three cows when the buffalo went away last year." The chief walked around, looked at Melissa, then came to a halt in front of Slocum.

"Your squaw?"

"I am *not*!" she blurted out.

"My squaw," Slocum said, drowning her out. "She is under my protection."

This quieted her, but Melissa simmered. Slocum hoped the pot wouldn't boil over and get them both in really hot water.

"She has fire. You should cut out her tongue."

"The chief of the Cree is a wise man in many ways," Slocum said. He shot Melissa a hard look to keep her silent.

A rapid fire of words from a half-dozen braves across the camp put Slocum on edge, but the chief nodded.

"You are welcome to share our food and fire. My brother's son speaks well of you saving his life."

"Do tell," Slocum said, wondering at that. He cast a quick look at Melissa, silently ordering her to stay quiet yet again. "We need to dry our clothing. Crossing the river to bring your brother's son to you has left us freezing."

The chief nodded but said nothing. Slocum knew that this was a crucial moment. He moved to Melissa and took her arm before she could explode with her opinions about how to be treated, what had to be done, and her demand that the Cree tell where Stringfellow and his gang held her boss captive.

She tried to pull away but Slocum kept up the pressure until she subsided.

"You will use my tipi."

"You honor me," Slocum said.

"Where will I stay?" Melissa yelped when Slocum tightened his grip on her again. "Stop that."

"Your squaw needs to be trained," the chief said.

"Once more you show your wisdom."

Slocum pulled her along with the horses and shoved her toward the oval opening in the hide tent. Melissa hit the ground and scampered inside on her hands and knees. Slocum followed, then pulled the flap shut behind them.

"How dare you let him call me a squaw!"

"You want to leave your scalp hanging at his belt? These are the Cree I told you about. The Blood tribe."

"They are peaceable enough."

"Because I brought back the chief's nephew while he was still alive and kicking. I saved your life."

"You—" Melissa sputtered and moved to the far side of the fire, sat cross-legged, and crossed her arms over her chest.

Slocum began stripping off his wet clothing. Sticks shoved into the dirt provided hangers for him to put the clothing near enough the fire to dry out. He kicked out of his boots and moved them where they would dry slowly, then put his gun belt, coat, vest, shirt, and jeans on the sticks.

He glanced at the woman. She hadn't budged. The ice on her dress melted and ran off to form a small mud puddle around her. He couldn't help laughing at her drowned rat look.

"What's so funny?"

"From the way you're sitting, you might as well be a castle with a moat around it."

Melissa looked down, saw the circle of water, then smiled a little. Then she looked up, her eyes going wide.

"What are you doing?"

"My longjohns are soaked, too. I'm going to dry them out." He skinned out of the wooly undergarment and strung it between two sticks.

He scooted around, naked as a jaybird, and stretched out on the chief's blanket. The fire felt good but parts of him were still cold.

"Are you going to spend the night like that?"

"There's only one blanket. Are you going to spend the night like that?"

She shivered, then looked up at him as he stretched out lean and naked.

"I could use a bit of warming up," she said, beginning to unfasten her coat. She hung it up and then worked to free her dress from around her shoulders.

Slocum watched with increasing interest as more bare, wet skin was revealed. She looked coyly over her shoulder, then wiggled some, causing her breasts to jiggle as she pulled free of her dress and was naked to the waist. With a move Slocum didn't quite follow because he was so absorbed with the sight of the firelight dancing on her white breasts, she sat, spun about, and got free of her dress. Hanging it near his clothing, she turned to him. Only her petticoats remained.

"Those look like they're weighing you down, all wet the way they are."

"They're not all that's wet," she said, moving her hands over her tits, down her belly, and vanishing under the band of the petticoats. She closed her eyes and shivered. Slocum saw this time it wasn't from the cold. He wanted to explore where her fingers already scouted.

With a tug, he had the last vestiges of her clothing pulled around the flare of her ass and down her legs. He cast the wet garment aside. He was getting hard, and taking proper care to dry out the petticoats held no interest for him. Not like the fleecy dark patch between her legs.

The fire flickered and spat out sparks. One arched like a comet and landed on the woman's bare belly. Slocum pounced on it to keep her flawless skin from blistering. He kissed the spot. A tiny hot spot burned into his tongue. This spurred him on.

He worked down from her navel to the tangled forest between her thighs. His tongue lashed out. She started to say something, but his quick movements, using only the top of his tongue, canceled her words and replaced them with tiny moans of joy.

When he shoved his fingers deep into her, she lay back on the blanket, arched up off the ground, and tried to grind herself into his face. He moved about, licking and kissing as he went. The nether lips provided oily moistness from deep within her body, but he left them to lightly kiss her tender inner thighs. From the way she thrashed about, he was tormenting muscles sore from riding. His hands cupped her buttocks. He felt the inflamed flesh. She'd had more than her share of misery riding with a backside so abused.

He rolled her onto her belly and gave her a light swat on her rump.

"That hurts!"

"As much as this?" He dived down and kissed the spot where his hand print burned in her white skin. Her answer was a cry of pure desire. He continued kissing and licking, then worked his hands between her thighs and pressed hard enough to let her know what he wanted.

Still facedown on the blanket, she spread her legs for him. He dropped down on top, positioned his hips, and slipped forward. The hard tip of his manhood stroked along the liquid crease that led to her heated core. Back and forth he moved, arousing her even more. When he finally pistoned forward and sank balls deep in her, she cried out in stark passion.

He held himself up on his hands on either side of her body. Melissa lifted her midsection off the blanket and worked back into his groin. They fit together perfectly. The curve of her ass might have been designed for the circle of his loins. Together they began moving. It took a few tries to finally reach an accommodation.

She lifted. He thrust. She ground her hips down around the fleshy spike hidden away inside. Then he withdrew and she sagged back, only to rise once more as he thrust forward.

Slocum bent and kissed the nape of her neck, her ear, her

cheek as he pistoned with greater need. The heat burning deep in his balls began to cause an ache that could not be denied. He moved faster, thrust deeper, worked about like a spoon stirring in a mixing bowl. He closed his eyes and absorbed all the sensations around him.

The mix of womanly scents with wood smoke, pine, and stark arousal turned him even harder within her. Heat from her depths charred his manhood even as the nearby fire burned at his back. Friction from movement added to the fuel feeding the conflagration growing within. He no longer resisted and spewed forth. He caught at the woman's shoulders for balance. She gasped, arched her back, shoulders rising as her hips went hard down into the blanket.

For a moment, they hung together, hot and joined, alone in the world. And then Slocum began to melt. Melissa sank forward and put her cheek on her crossed arms as he slid away and came to lie beside her.

"I suspected you were better than out at the pond," she said in a soft voice. "I was right."

"The fire heated everything up," he said.

He stroked over her bare back, lingering a moment on the curves of her buttocks. His fingers slid between her legs and rested in the pink crease he found there. Tiny twitches told him she was enjoying this as much as he was.

"Is the Indian chief going to help us find Rory?" She moved onto her side so she could press her backside against him spoon fashion.

Slocum almost sat upright. The question irritated him. All she thought about was Rory Randolph.

"I suppose I can make a deal with him," he said.

"What kind of deal?"

"He thinks you're my squaw. I saw the way he looked at you. He'd trade any information for another squaw, especially one like you."

"What are you saying? You can't be serious!" She tried to get away.

Slocum was tuckered out after the day, after the love-making.

"Real serious. Might even get a couple ponies as well as where Stringfellow is hiding out."

He smiled and drifted off to sleep. When he awoke hours later, Melissa had disappeared. He sat up, saw her clothes were nowhere to be seen, and then cursed. She had believed him when he joked about trading her to the Cree chieftain.

11

Slocum slipped into his clothes, all nice and warm from drying by the fire. His boots were still wet, but he had endured worse. The whole time he dressed, he cursed Melissa and her pigheaded determination to find Randolph. As he strapped on his gun belt, a small smile came to his lips, then faded. He shouldn't have joshed her about selling her to the Cree. She was an Easterner and couldn't know he was joking. As much trouble as she made for him now, he ought to have gone ahead and made the deal. Let the Cree chief deal with her.

He crawled from the tent and stood, stretching. Dawn turned the rim of the eastern mountains a gold that quickly changed as the sun rose. The Cree bustled about camp, doing chores and preparing for another day of hunting food before the heavy snows came.

The chief came over and waited until Slocum acknowledged him.

"She left. Did you send her away?"

Slocum shook his head. Explaining Melissa's motives

was beyond the chief's command of English. Hell, it was beyond Slocum's.

"She hunts for . . . another," he said lamely. Explaining her need to find her boss without lying eluded Slocum. "It is a revenge she must deliver to an enemy who has wronged her and her clan."

This made sense to the Cree. It almost made sense to Slocum, although the trouble Randolph found himself in was of his own doing. Why Melissa felt so strongly about pulling his chestnuts from the fire came down to how she must have made a promise to the writer. A man's word—or a woman's—had to be kept, though Slocum had never seen that kind of relationship between her and Randolph.

"You will go after her?"

"I must," Slocum said. Continuing the lie, he added, "She's my squaw and her fight is mine."

"So it is."

Slocum hesitated to ask, but he had to. Without knowing what direction Melissa had fled in the night, he had no way of ever tracking her down. She had some idea where Stringfellow had camped and thought Randolph was being held there, but Slocum was turned around after crossing the river in the night. Melissa's sense of direction in the wilderness could never match his own. Luck might take her back in the right direction, but the odds were against that. Even seasoned explorers died in these mountains relying on luck rather than knowledge.

The Cree chief waited for Slocum to speak his piece.

"I cannot find her by myself. Will the Cree hunters help me find her?"

"And kill the one she seeks?"

"His name is Stringfellow and he leads an outlaw gang. They are killers, dangerous desperados. Do you know of him from your scouting in these here parts?"

The chief pondered for a while, then said, "Lost Horse

might know. He hunts in the direction where you were found."

"Is Lost Horse the brave who was shot?"

The chief nodded once.

"He cannot be well enough to ride. If he told me what he knows, I can seek out Stringfellow on my own."

The chief turned and walked off. Slocum was slow to follow as they went to a tipi decorated with mystical symbols. The chief stood back and motioned for Slocum to enter. He ducked and went inside, coughing when he sucked in the thick smoke billowing from a pot filled with boiling green liquid.

The medicine man glared at him, shook a rattle, and subsided when the chief entered. Propped up on a pile of blankets, the man Slocum had shot watched him alertly.

"You did not kill me."

"There was no reason to," Slocum said. "What happened was a mistake. We are not enemies."

"We are brothers." The man held out his hand. Slocum clasped his forearm. The medicine man grunted and left, shaking his rattle as he went outside. The sound faded as he stalked off. "What does my brother need from me?"

Slocum glanced at the chief. There had been some discussion between them earlier, it seemed.

Slocum explained his need to find "his squaw" and help her bring justice down on the head of Will Stringfellow.

"Have you seen a band of road agents? White men robbing stagecoaches and travelers along the roads?"

"There is a camp a day's ride away. They scare away deer and elk, so we avoid them."

"That is wise. They would shoot you out of hand."

Lost Horse started to speak, fire coming to his eyes, then he subsided. Slocum saw he would have to avoid reminding the Indian how he had come to get laid up. It took all his willpower not to reach over and touch the butt of his Colt.

"Is there loot?"

"For a great warrior, there will be. These men steal everything they can find."

"Not gold or silver. Do they have horses? Guns?"

"If we find Stringfellow, you can have his and his gang's horses, guns, and supplies."

"You want only revenge?"

Slocum had grown easy with the lie that this was all he wanted. Randolph might get caught up in a big fight and killed. Dealing with the Cree if this happened wasn't anything he'd anticipated. Randolph had to look after himself. All Slocum wanted was to get the woman out of the middle of a gunfight and on a train back East, where she belonged. If Randolph went along with her, fine. If he ended up as a coyote's dinner, he had brought it on himself by poking Stringfellow with a stick like he was a caged animal.

"Only revenge."

"But you would keep any gold or silver this Stringfellow has stolen?" Lost Horse kept his face impassive, but Slocum knew what went on behind those dark eyes.

"I don't care about the money. Take it. Leave it. All that matters is revenge."

Slocum worried that Lost Horse would press on the reason for seeking revenge, but he settled back.

"We leave soon."

Slocum knew better than to ask if the brave was up to travel. That would insult him. From what he had seen, Lost Horse was fit enough for the trail. Whether he would be much of an ally in a fight with Stringfellow and his men was another matter, but Slocum wasn't inclined to use a frontal assault. The outlaw had a half-dozen men with him. Killing a couple had reduced their number, but they still outnumbered and outgunned any attackers. However he fought Stringfellow, it had to be done from hiding.

The chance existed that he and Stringfellow would never square off in another gunfight. If Melissa could be corralled and sent packing, the outlaw could keep on robbing and killing all he wanted.

"I'll get ready." Slocum left the chief with Lost Horse. The two exchanged lengthy arguments Slocum couldn't follow.

He stepped out into the warm morning sun. It took him less time than he thought to find his pinto, feed and water it, then be sure what supplies he carried were securely lashed behind the saddle. He wasn't surprised to see Lost Horse ride up. The sight of the chief and a dozen braves made him ask.

"Are they all coming to hunt Stringfellow?"

"They ride part of the way," Lost Horse said. "We do not give up our hunt for game. If our scouts find your enemy, good. If they find food, good."

Slocum stepped up into the saddle and looked around.

"I am sure the woman lit out looking for Stringfellow. If we find her trail, this will lead to the outlaw."

"How is it your squaw knows where your enemy is and you do not?"

"She has a map."

This caused the Indians to exchange more words.

The chief rode over until he faced Slocum. "This map shows such things?"

"My squaw thinks it does. It shows elevations, valleys, and rivers."

"And where your enemy camps?"

Slocum knew what the chief was angling for, so he beat him to asking outright.

"When we find Stringfellow, you can have the map showing all this." He swept his arm around to encompass the mountains and everything within sight. "It will be a great help for you, as you move your camp with the seasons. Your tribe will look up to you as a wise and great leader."

Slocum saw the smile and knew he had enlisted the man's aid for the hunt. But finding Melissa was more important than locating Stringfellow's camp. He started paying attention not to the ground where they rode but to the horizon. Now and then he caught sight of a ridge where the view improved. Each time, however, he failed to spot the woman. The thick forests hindered real searching. Many leaves had fallen from the oak and maple, but at this altitude the juniper, pine, and spruce trees provided a complete shield of movement.

In late afternoon, Lost Horse lifted his chin and silently pointed. For a moment Slocum stared off into the distance, not seeing what the Cree already had. Then he heaved a sigh of relief.

"Your squaw rides in circles."

Slocum saw how this was possible. If Melissa took one branching canyon, she ended up where she started. Taking the other branch circled about and also left her where she started. The only way out of the circular track was to climb one canyon wall or simply retreat and find a different route. With her map, she should have seen how futile her current efforts were.

"I'll see to her," he said. "You wait here until I signal. Seeing you might spook her."

Slocum wasn't sure if Melissa was armed, but if she carried a hideout pistol, the sight of the Cree could set her off and begin an exchange of lead that would end badly for her. He wasn't even sure if he popped up that she wouldn't shoot him. After all, she thought he had sold her to the chief.

He made his way down a ravine, using the banks to protect himself on either side, then worked his way up an embankment and across a small stream before coming out in the mouth of the tangle of canyons where Melissa found herself trapped.

He came within a hundred yards of her before she spotted him, and then only because she once more came from a branching canyon to return to the beginning of her labyrinth.

"Don't run," Slocum called. "You're going in circles, no matter which way you ride. I've watched you for a couple hours."

"You sold me to that . . . to that red man!"

"I was pulling your leg because you were being such a pain."

"That wasn't what you said after you . . . you raped me!"

Slocum sighed and kept riding, wary of her being armed. She started to ride away, but her horse balked. It had tired during the circuits through the canyon and needed to rest.

"You gave as good as you got," he said. "It's going to be dark in another hour. You intend to stay lost?"

"I'm not lost. I have my map."

"Why hasn't it shown you you're wasting your time and riding in circles?"

"There's supposed to be a way out of the canyon, at the back, but I can't find it."

"How old's the map?" Slocum kept a steady walk up to a spot a few yards from her. "Show me what went wrong."

"It's here, right here." She held up the map and caught the slanting afternoon sun. "The map is only three years old. It was done by a U.S. Survey Team sent from Washington by the army. They weren't country bumpkins. They were professionals and knew how to properly record what they found."

"Including a canyon wall collapsing sometime between when they drew the map and now?"

"Rock fall? But—"

"Why were you so intent on getting through here? Is Stringfellow's camp nearby?" He didn't say "supposed to be" even though he doubted Melissa actually knew where the gang camped.

"It ought to be a mile or two that way. That's where I wrote it using this very map."

Slocum looked hard at her, then over his shoulder as Lost Horse and the chief rode up.

Melissa fumbled the map and dug around in her skirts.

"Hold on," Slocum said, riding closer and grabbing the map. "They're on our side."

"They want me sexually. They—"

"They aren't our enemies. Remember that Stringfellow still has your boss. The Cree can help us find them."

She didn't relax as Lost Horse rode closer, his hand on a six-shooter shoved into his waistband.

Slocum held up the map and motioned to the chief. He showed less caution than his brave. Almost reverently Slocum handed over the topographic map. The Indian took it and turned it around and around, then stared at Slocum.

"What is this?"

Slocum showed where they were on the map, described how the closeness of the rings determined altitude. The closer together they were, the steeper the terrain until the smallest circles gave the mountain peaks. The chief slowly began to smile, then eagerly point out hills and valleys around them according to the elevation.

"Your camp is here," Slocum said, tracing from their location back to the site.

Lost Horse made a chopping motion with his hand. The chief started to rebuke him for the interruption, but Lost Horse continued until the chief folded the map and tucked it under his buckskin shirt.

"That's my map. You can't give it to this savage!"

"Quiet," Slocum said.

"I need it to find Rory!"

"Is the outlaw camp through there?" Slocum pointed down the canyon.

"You must climb over rock wall. It is easier to ride there and circle about," Lost Horse said. He spoke rapidly with his chief again. Then he said, "We must leave. They come."

"Who? The cavalry?"

"Posse from the town." Lost Horse clenched his fist and tapped it against his chest. Slocum duplicated the gesture, but he doubted the Indian saw it. He was galloping off with the chief.

As they rode, several others joined them.

"What are they talking about? If that's Stringfellow coming for us, we need to find a place to ambush him. Then we can rescue Rory and—"

Slocum ignored her. He guessed distances and how much light they had left.

"If we ride hard, and Lost Horse wasn't misleading us, we can reach Stringfellow's camp before sundown. Do we stand around and argue or do we ride?"

Melissa answered by riding off. Slocum trailed her, watching for any sign of the riders Lost Horse had mentioned. They skirted the canyons and came into a valley. As much as Slocum hated to admit it, Melissa had been right about the location of the outlaws' camp. If they hadn't taken a detour getting Lost Horse back to his tribe, they would have come on Stringfellow the day before.

But they wouldn't have spent such a delightful night. Slocum scratched himself as he remembered how it had been with Melissa. She was a pretty filly, but he couldn't figure her out. The coupling seemed something she did as a favor or a way of persuading him to do what she wanted. As long as he wanted to do it, too, he saw nothing wrong with this. But he had to wonder about her and Randolph. When she said she wasn't screwing her boss, it carried a hint of truth to it. Slocum had to ask himself why this was the least bit plausible when she willingly spread her knees for him to keep him as an ally.

"There's the overhang. Oh, I wish you hadn't given away the map. It would be useful now deciding how to approach the camp."

"Quiet."

"Don't you tell me—"

He clamped his hand over her mouth, then grabbed her with his other hand to prevent her from pulling away.

"Listen. Use your ears, not your mouth, for once."

Melissa subsided when she heard what Slocum already had. Her eyes went wide. Only then did he release her.

"We've got riders coming up from the right."

"And from behind you," came a voice he recognized.

Slocum swung about in the saddle, his hand going to his six-shooter.

"Don't think on it, Slocum. It's not worth the fuss."

Slocum stared down the twin barrels of a shotgun.

12

"You have some reason to point that scattergun at me, Marshal?" Slocum kept his hands well away from his sides and the Colt Navy.

"I wanted to be sure you weren't spooked. I ought to have knowed better." Marshal Lennox lowered the shotgun. He called out, "Come on in, boys. Nothing to worry on here."

Slocum saw ten men come from the shadows. He and Melissa had walked smack into an ambush and hadn't even known it. Whether she had distracted him or he was getting sloppy hardly mattered. If this had been Stringfellow and his gang, he would have been filled full of holes and Melissa would be their prisoner.

"Sorry," he said to the woman.

She started to speak, then clamped her mouth shut. At last. Slocum was glad for her silence. He had expected her to berate him and then light into the marshal for all the woes of the world. Either shock or sudden good sense kept her from such pointless complaints.

"What brings you out here, Marshal?"

"Same as you, 'less I miss my guess. How'd you know where the camp was?"

"A good guess on Miss Benton's part," he said. Slocum doubted she would argue that since she had been hell bound for this spot. He didn't want her mentioning the Cree. That would only complicate matters, and explaining how he had enlisted the tribe's aid did nothing to bring Stringfellow to justice.

"Now how'd a city lady figure Stringfellow would camp here?"

"Go on, tell him, Melissa." Slocum waited for her to explain that. He was as interested in the answer as the marshal. If she kept the Indians and the topographic map out of it, they were both better served.

"I . . . I found a scrap of paper with a crude map on it. One of the outlaws must have dropped it when Mr. Randolph was kidnapped."

"That's right convenient," Lennox said. "Me and the posse had to arrive here the hard way."

"Little Joe told you?" Slocum smiled when he saw the marshal's expression.

"Something like that. I made a deal with him. When Stringfellow and those still riding with him are caught, he gets a horse and a day's head start."

Slocum knew that Lennox would never go after Little Joe Barkhausen if he had bigger fish to fry. Little Joe had to know that, too, which made his information all the more likely to be true.

"What else is there, Marshal? There's something more that brought you out here." Melissa stepped closer to get a good look at the marshal's face in the dark.

"Why'd you say that, Miss Benton?"

"Those men riding with you aren't from Idaho Falls."

Slocum took a closer look at the men nearest to him. She was right. The local residents dressed like wranglers and even miners in canvas trousers with checked plaid flannel shirts. These men were dressed enough alike to be part of an army.

"Railroad dicks," Slocum said. "They all work for the railroad."

"A robbery! Will Stringfellow is planning to rob a train. Your prisoner ratted him out. That's worth being released. A few dollars in reward is nothing to capturing an entire gang, that's true, but protecting a train carrying something truly valuable is worth far more."

"Did you see their badges?" Lennox asked.

"I know their kind," Melissa said.

For some reason, Slocum believed her. She'd had no call ever to see a railroad bull and yet had spotted them before he had. The years he had spent out West included more than one stolen ride on a freight car. Getting onto a train going out of Saint Louis had proven hard for him. Two railroad detectives had pursued him for the better part of two hours until he had wedged himself under a cattle car and the train had pulled out. Riding the rails wasn't comfortable or even safe, not with the cinders and ties flashing by at thirty miles an hour inches from his back, but that had seemed the lesser of two evils. Being caught by the railroad bulls meant a severe beating if he was lucky and a slow death if he wasn't.

"How far off is Stringfellow's camp?" Lennox watched her like a hawk.

"I am sure it's on the far side of this copse."

"The night makes it hard finding the landmarks Little Joe mentioned," Lennox said. He stepped away and spoke at length with a man that might have been an ax-handle broad across the shoulders. The whispered exchange became more heated, but when Lennox returned, he didn't appear the least bit ruffled. "We're going to circle the camp and move in. You stay here with Slocum, Miss Benton. We don't want you getting shot in the dark."

"I can—"

"He means the railroad detectives are likely to shoot you out of hand," Slocum said. "They want a body count and don't much care whose body is included."

"They'd kill us? Me? Wait, no, you've got to realize why I came out here. Rory Randolph is a prisoner. Tell them not to gun him down."

"I'll let them know," the marshal said. He shot Slocum a hard look, then joined the detectives.

In seconds the night swallowed them up. Only the soft sound of wind slipping through tall pines remained. When Melissa began breathing harder, Slocum took notice of her. She pulled out a pad of paper none the worse for the dunking it must have taken in the river and scribbled furiously. The faster she wrote, the more excited she became, until he worried she might alert the outlaws.

"I know, John," she said, not looking up as she flipped to a fresh page. "Those railroad men are killers, no better than Stringfellow and his gang. Some of them were possibly train robbers before they were deputized."

"I'm glad you understand how the railroads hire their private armies. Are you writing a letter to complain that Randolph might get himself killed along with the road agents?"

"What's that? Oh, this, never mind what I'm writing. Notes for Rory. We need to get closer so I can see how the attack builds."

Slocum frowned. By now there should have been gunfire. Other than Melissa's harsh, excited breathing and the scratch of her pencil on paper, he heard nothing. Even the wind had died. He slid his six-shooter from its holster. This got her attention.

"What's wrong? Oh, there isn't any shooting. The outlaws aren't in camp." She took a deep breath, then sighed. "They might have killed Rory. I cannot believe they would leave him tied up and unguarded in their camp."

"I can't imagine why Stringfellow kidnapped him at all," Slocum said. "If he was mad, a man like Stringfellow takes out his mad with his fists or guns. He ripped up the book. That's what he'd want to do with its author."

"Torture. Do you think he intends to torture Rory? How would he do that? Do you know some secret Indian techniques?"

Slocum had been captive of the Apaches, easily the cruelest of the Indians he'd had the misfortune to cross. There was nothing secret about the ways they had found to inflict pain. Some might have been copied from the white men, but most of them were well known among the Apaches and their enemies—which counted for most all tribes.

"You stay. I'll find out what is going on."

"You're not leaving me behind! I'm going with you. I want to see with my own eyes anything that's happened."

He set off without saying another word. Short of tying her up, he saw no way to keep her from trailing behind him. He made his way through the forest without making a sound. In comparison, Melissa might have been a stampeding herd of cattle. Slocum kept his attention focused ahead. He came to a railroad bull pressed behind a tree. Slocum called out to the man, hoping he wouldn't startle him into firing wildly. The man was experienced enough not to react that way.

He motioned for Slocum to approach.

"I smelled her," the man said. "Heard her, too, but she's wearing perfume."

Slocum had not noticed, but he knew his nose grew accustomed fast to any odor around him. Not even a slaughterhouse or an outhouse bothered him after the first whiff. Melissa's perfume might be nice but had became part of his background.

"Where's Stringfellow?" Slocum held out his hand to keep Melissa back as she tried to crowd forward.

"The boss can't find him. The marshal can't either."

This told Slocum that Lennox might think he led the posse but the real boss was one of the railroad men.

"Did they find Rory? Mr. Randolph? Did they find his

body?" Melissa crowded close behind Slocum. Her fingers cut into his arm so hard that he pulled away. "Were there any bodies in the camp?"

"I can't rightly say," the railroad detective said. "I was told to hang back and make certain nobody escaped, if they was lyin' doggo, waitin' for a chance to run for it."

"Come on," Slocum said, taking Melissa by the arm. He looked at the railroad detective. "It's all right. The boss won't mind."

"He's a mean one and a stickler for havin' his orders followed to the letter."

Slocum doubted the man would shoot them in the back. Still, the hair rose on his neck until they reached the edge of what had been a large encampment. Embers in three campfires lay cold now. In the dark he saw where Stringfellow had corralled his horses.

"There," Melissa said. "That's the overhang I saw on the map."

He looked up and saw a dark figure silhouetted against the stars walking along the edge of an abutment. A large outjut of rock joined the side of the mountain and gave refuge from the elements.

"Nothing, Sonny," called the man. "No trace of anybody."

"Come on down then," came a voice from across the camp.

The man Slocum identified as Sonny had several others from the posse gathered around. Where Marshal Lennox had gotten off to was a poser, but this man was the real leader.

"They held him here, John. I know it." Melissa stood under the rock ledge, turning in a complete circle. "Here. See? There's some rope about long enough to tie a man's hands behind his back."

He saw the rope but no hint as to how she got the other details. It didn't escape him that she might have made it all up.

"Slocum, over here."

He looked to his left. Lennox motioned for him to join

him. Slocum saw that Melissa had her pad out again and wrote away, holding it so close her nose almost brushed the paper. She would be occupied with her notes for some time from the way she concentrated.

"What'd you find, Marshal?"

"They rode out an hour or two before sundown. We missed them by a big margin."

"What do you make of the direction they rode? They didn't pass me as I came in." He started to mention the Cree but hesitated. If any of the tribe had seen Stringfellow, the alarm would have been raised immediately.

"I'm not sure of the territory but think this leads into a canyon that opens out on a long stretch of railroad coming through the hills. The grades are such that the train slows. That'd be a good place for Stringfellow to rob the train."

Slocum agreed. Stringfellow had a way of doing things. He had let the stagecoach go up a steep grade at Hangman's Hill before attacking. If the tactic worked on a stage, it had to work as well on a locomotive. All chance of racing away was removed.

"Who's the one giving the orders to the posse?" Slocum looked behind at Sonny.

"Sonny Briggs, come all the way from the home office. The owners of the 'road are fed up with the robberies, so they sent damned near a company of men."

"And Briggs is the one in charge."

"You figured out that I'm just along for the ride?"

"Miss Benton is worried about her boss."

"I haven't seen hide nor hair of Randolph," the marshal said. "It's a good thing I'm here because those gents would as soon kill him as look at him if that got them an inch closer to catching Stringfellow."

"The whole gang rode for the notch in the hills where the train slows?"

"I've got to tell Sonny. He's the one payin' my salary out here."

"What reward's the railroad offering for Stringfellow's head?"

"One thousand dollars for the entire gang. I couldn't pin Sonny down if all of them had to be killed or locked up before the money was paid or if it was only for Stringfellow."

"The railroad detectives have found no trace of Rory," Melissa said as she made her way through the dark. "Mr. Briggs thinks they took him along with them to use as a hostage."

"Hostage?" Lennox snorted in contempt. "You don't think they're gonna hold a gun to Randolph's head and make the engineer stop, do you? The train crew won't know him from Adam."

"What if they tied him to the tracks?" Melissa hesitated, wanting to reach for her pad and pencil again as this new idea came to her. "They tie him to the tracks, the engineer stops the train, the outlaws then commandeer the engine and thereby put the whole train at their mercy."

"Mighty imaginative," Lennox said. "If they try to rob the train in the dark, there's not an engineer on any route that could see a man tied down on the tracks in time. They don't put cowcatchers on the front for nothing."

"I don't understand," Melissa said.

"What the marshal is saying is that wildlife and cattle get on the tracks all the time. The engineer doesn't slow. Full speed ahead might work better since the impact knocks the animal up on the cowcatcher and off to one side."

"Slocum's right. They don't have to stop if there's no meat caught on the front."

"Unless the engineer and fireman get hungry," Sonny Briggs said loudly. "Then they might have themselves a good steak cooked right on the firebox. The line supervisors try to keep that from happening but on long trips a man gets powerful hungry."

"The train would smash right into a man?" Melissa spoke with a catch in her voice.

"A man? The engineer'd never notice a man in the dark."

"Poor Rory," Melissa said.

"How far are the tracks from here?" Slocum asked.

"A couple hours' ride," Lennox said. "In the dark, more than that if we get lost."

"The train would be crossing the pass before dawn," Sonny said, peering at a railroad timetable while one of his henchmen held up a match so he could read it. "Yeah, that's right, if the train keeps to the schedule."

"Stringfellow has something in mind," Slocum said. "He might pull up a rail."

"Derail the train," Melissa said.

Again the catch of excitement came to her voice. "That would be spectacular. The boiler might burst and spray steam and hot water everywhere."

"More likely a threat would be the firebox splittin'," said Lennox. "The whole damned mountain could be set on fire. With winter comin' at us like it is, there are dead leaves and dried branches everywhere."

"A fire'd shut down this line for days. Weeks," Sonny Briggs said. "Men! Mount up. We're riding through the night!"

Grumbles greeted the order, but Slocum saw all the railroad bulls ride out within minutes in a single-file line like cavalry troopers. He, the marshal, and Melissa were left behind.

"We can't let them find Stringfellow first, John. Marshal Lennox! We have to save Rory. Those railroad policemen won't care what happens to him even if he's tied up and Stringfellow's prisoner."

"She's got a point, Marshal." Slocum turned to get his horse.

"Don't be in such a hurry. I might just know a shortcut," Lennox said. "Those boys are going down the main canyon. Stringfellow went that way because he wasn't in any hurry. My way is a mite tighter and more difficult but can get us to the pass an hour before them."

"I so wish you hadn't given my map to—"

Slocum cut her off.

"How much tighter are you talking, Marshal?"

"You got any fear of havin' rocks fall on your head or gettin' crushed?"

"You said you weren't familiar with this area." Slocum watched the lawman's face. A tiny smile came to his lips. "That's not exactly right, is it?"

"I've been huntin' up here a passel of times over the years. Best deer hunting in Idaho. I saw one of Sonny's boys listenin' real hard to what we said and saw no reason to let the railroad dicks know everything I know."

"What are we waiting for?" Melissa asked. "Let's ride. Please, Marshal, we still have to hurry. Stringfellow has a considerable start on us."

"But if he's intent on robbin' the train," the marshal told her, "he's goin' be right where we can find him, waitin' as long as it takes. What worries me more is Sonny bein' wrong about when the train is scheduled to come through the pass."

From the way the leader of the railroad bulls had worked on the schedule, he wasn't likely to be far wrong. If anything, the train might be delayed farther east, causing them all to wait.

"Did you find anything of interest in the camp?" Slocum asked.

"Not a thing."

"That's about what I thought," Slocum said. "It'll take us fifteen minutes to get our horses and join you."

"I won't start without you," Lennox said. "Where we're goin', I'm goin' to need all the help I can get."

Slocum quickly found out that the marshal wasn't joking.

13

Melissa cried out as rock tumbled down on her.

"Quiet. If you keep shoutin' like that, you're goin' to bring the whole damned mountainside down on our heads." Lennox halted at the front of the single-file line and glared back at her.

Slocum brought up the rear and had seen the rocks begin to tumble, disturbed by their passage, but hadn't warned her in time. He threw up his arm to protect his face from the dust. The worst of the rock fall had descended on Melissa's head.

"Help me get free, dammit," the woman flared.

Lennox kept moving. Slocum had to assist her since the narrow crevice prevented him from getting around her. His shoulders rubbed either side of the passage. When he reached her, he had to quiet his pinto. The horse was finally spooked by the closeness and dust. Only when the horse was settled did he turn his attention to Melissa.

She stood stock-still, her face brown with dirt. He expected to see tears running down her cheeks and leaving muddy tracks. Instead, she got mad. Her lips pulled back like a feral animal's, and she savagely threw the bits of rock

she could lift from in front of her to behind, stopping Slocum's advance.

"I can't reach you if you block my way."

"Go to hell. How do we know he's leading us in the right
direction? I'm so turned around that we might be in the
Andes by now instead of near railroad tracks." She cursed
some more, then sat on a rock and shook with anger. "For
two cents I'd leave him."

Slocum wanted to point out the reason they were scraping through narrow rock chimneys and stumbling along
these tight passages wasn't to save Rory Randolph. The
writer was almost certainly dead. They wanted to stop
Stringfellow and his gang. Randolph's death was just another
charge to be levied against the outlaw. Instead of time in
some prison, Will Stringfellow would swing for his crimes.

"I'll move the stones past and between my horse's legs,"
Slocum said. He worked blind, but the sharp-edged stones
told him what had to be done. His back ached and his eyes
watered by the time he got his horse past the rock fall.

Melissa had gone ahead. He had lost sight of the marshal,
but the man had either exited the passage or found his way
to the center of the earth. Either possibility was fine with
Slocum. He didn't get all nervous and flighty in tight spaces,
but the crevices the marshal had led them through in the
dark matched being buried alive. Slocum had refrained from
making this comparison to Melissa, not wanting to scare her.

Still, her reaction made him think better of her. She
wasn't bawling. She was fighting mad. That would get them
all through the mountains just fine.

He felt sudden cross drafts and knew he had left the rock
crevice.

"Down there," Lennox said. "You can't see the tracks in
the dark, but you can make out the pass where the railroad
runs."

"Moonlight just reflected off a steel rail," Melissa said.
"I can make out the tracks!"

This set her to writing again on her pad. Slocum wanted to see what she found so important that every free instant set her to penning some new observation.

"We got here a good hour before Sonny and his men," Lennox said, a touch of pride in his voice.

"If the train's not here, how are we going to flush String-fellow? You're right about how dark it is," Slocum said. "And moonlight's not reflecting off the outlaws."

"This is the spot where the grade turns steepest before reaching the summit, maybe as much as three percent. It's a gentle slope once through the pass. That makes us about where Stringfellow will try to stop the train."

"I'm so tuckered out, I couldn't fight a newborn kitten," Slocum said. He sat on a rock, then shook all over. Dust flew in all directions. "I want to know where the outlaws are before I ride down there. Otherwise, it's like charging smack dab into a firing squad."

"You saw enough of that during the war," Lennox said. "Fact is, I did, too."

"You hardly look old enough to have been in the war, Marshal," Melissa said.

"I enlisted in place of my older brother. I was twelve. He had a gimpy leg but they were goin' to take him anyway."

Slocum heard nothing of the South in the man's words. He doubted they had ever faced each other across a battle-ground, but he didn't want to open old wounds.

Melissa went to pull out her paper again. Slocum stood and tried to look over her shoulder. She jerked away as if he had set fire to her hair.

"I want to see what you think is so all-fired important to keep writing down."

"It's nothing," she said. "Mind your own business."

"That's mighty hard when you consider why I'm out here. If anything, I'd say I'm taking care of your business—or Randolph's."

He started to take the pad from her hands, but she pushed

him away. His own anger flared. He had ridden through rocky passages so tight he felt like he was in a grave, he was dirty and hungry and tired, and he wanted to see what she was writing. Before he could force her to show him, Lennox let out a hiss like steam escaping from a locomotive pressure valve.

"The train's comin'," he said. "Hear it?"

At first Slocum didn't. Then the deep rumble echoed off the distant rock walls in the pass. He drew his six-shooter, checked to be sure it was clean of grit, then stuffed it back into his holster.

"I'm ready. Where's the best place for us?"

"Miss Benton, stay here. Me and Slocum'll go to the floor of the pass. We're almost at the summit so Stringfellow and his gang will attack the train a couple hundred yards down the slope."

Slocum swung onto his pony and started down the rocky slope behind Lennox. When he heard stones tumbling behind him, he started to shout at Melissa to get back to safety. The report of a dozen guns firing drowned out his orders.

"There they are! 'Bout where I thought," cried the marshal. He put his heels to his horse and shot off. He pulled his rifle from the sheath at his knee, cocked it, and started firing as he rode.

Slocum wasn't much farther behind. He paid no attention to Melissa. If she didn't have the sense God gave a goose to stay safely back, that was her problem. He drew his pistol and galloped along the tracks. When he got close enough to see two dark figures alongside the tracks, he opened fire. His first shot was the lucky one. The outlaw let out a screech and keeled over. The next four rounds scared the other train robber but didn't wing him. The nearness of his rounds drove the man back from the tracks, which Slocum counted as almost as good. Take as many of the outlaws from the fight as possible.

He had one shot left before he would pull out his own

rifle. He leveled his pistol as an outlaw climbed up the side
of the engine. The muzzle flash from the outlaw's six-gun
illuminated his face an instant before the fireman tumbled
off the far side of the engine, the outlaw's bullet in his chest.

Slocum had the man squarely in his sights and still
missed. Surprise had caused him to jerk the trigger, pulling
the weapon off its target. Then he found himself ducking as
other outlaws drew a bead on him.

Slocum bent low and wheeled about, racing away from
the fight. He heard Lennox's rifle barking repeatedly,
answered by the duller pops from the outlaws' six-shooters.
Only when he was far enough up the hill that he was out of
range did he turn and stare back at the fight.

"You can't leave him," cried Melissa. "The marshal is
fighting all by himself."

"I saw one of the gang gun down the fireman," he said.
"So?"

He looked up at her. Dawn began to bring light to a new
day. He saw her expression of anger in the dim light change
to one of horror when he told her what he had seen.

"You're mistaken. You have to be!"

"I'm not wrong. That was Randolph who pulled the trigger. He's joined Stringfellow's gang."

"I don't care if that's President Grant holdin' up the
train," shouted Lennox. "I'm goin' to stop the lot of them!"

With that, the marshal turned back and rejoined the fight.
By now the outlaws had taken over the locomotive and held
the engineer at gunpoint. The train had ground to a halt.

"John, it's not true. Why are you lying?"

Slocum reloaded, looked at her with pity and a touch of
anger, then spurred his pinto back downhill in the direction
of the train. With his own eyes, he had seen Randolph kill
the fireman. Trying to sort all this out could wait. Laying
down supporting fire for the marshal might save both their
lives since Lennox was bound and determined to take on
the entire gang by himself.

"We got to fall back, Slocum," the marshal yelled. "They got the iron plate of the engine to protect them."

He fired a few times. His rifle bullets spanged off the thick sides of the cab. Stringfellow popped up now and then to fire back. When Slocum was beginning to think his eyes had deceived him before, he saw Randolph peer around the side and send a slug in the marshal's direction. Slocum fired and drove the writer back to cover, giving Lennox time to dismount and drop under the coal tender.

"Get out of there!" Slocum saw that the marshal had trapped himself between Stringfellow and Randolph up front and the rest of the gang behind.

Men came up on either side of the train. Those on Slocum's side drove him to cover in some rocks a dozen yards away. He pulled out his rifle. At this range his six-shooter was nothing more than a noisemaker. Already the thunder of guns firing about deafened him. The reports rattled off the high, sloping walls of the pass and echoed away. He added to the cacophony with steady fire directed at those sneaking up on the marshal. For his part, Lennox knew how dangerous his position had become but could do nothing to save himself.

If he tried to move forward, Stringfellow would shoot him. But staying where he lay under the coal car meant the rest of the gang would flush him out in a few seconds.

Slocum had only a few seconds to freely pick his targets. He winged one outlaw and sighted in on another when windows in the leading passenger car were busted out and three outlaws thrust their rifles through and took aim at him. Driven back behind the rock, he knew Lennox had only seconds of life left.

"Get 'em, boys. Don't worry about capturing any of the bastards!"

Slocum chanced a look around the rock, flinched as a bullet ricocheted off in front of his face, and then he let out a cheer. Sonny Briggs and his railroad detectives had finally made it through the canyons and joined the fight. If it had been one-sided in favor of the outlaws before, their advantage vanished in a flash.

The three outlaws in the passenger car found themselves pinned down now. Two of the posse fired and forced them to stay low as others went in from the front and rear. More glass exploded outward as the fight narrowed to the three train robbers. And then there was nothing but ominous silence.

"Back to the mail car," Briggs ordered. "Secure the vault and keep the mail safe."

Lennox rolled out from under the coal tender but paid no attention to the posse rushing toward the rear of the train. His eyes fixed on the engine. Slocum had not seen Stringfellow go down in the fusillade unleashed by Briggs's men. And he quickly saw there was a good reason for that. Will Stringfellow popped up like a prairie dog and fired three times at Lennox.

The marshal twisted and dropped to one knee. He had been hit, but Slocum saw it wasn't a serious injury. Leaving his safety behind the rock, he walked toward Stringfellow, firing methodically. Every round was intended to bring down the gang leader.

The shots drove Stringfellow back to the safety of the engine. Slocum rushed to the marshal's side and pulled him upright.

"You hit bad?"

"Hardly nicked me, but it burns like hell," Lennox said. He took his hand away from his thigh. The denim had been shot away but only a little blood oozed out.

"Just a crease," Slocum said. "Can you walk?"

"Hell and damnation, man, I can do better than that. I can fight! I'm not about to give up when I'm this close to catching those sons of bitches."

They pressed against the side of the coal tender, then

edged forward. Slocum motioned to the marshal that he was going to make a move and wanted covering fire. Lennox gripped his six-shooter and nodded.

Slocum spun out and fired. The bullet bounced around inside the cab, bringing a cry of pain and fury. When he didn't get return fire, Slocum jumped up on the metal rungs and kicked hard, flopping onto his belly. Lennox swarmed up behind him. Both of them had their six-guns trained on the engineer. Otherwise, the cab was empty.

"They done left, you idiots," the engineer grated out. He struggled to sit up as he held his left arm.

"Help him, Slocum." Lennox slid on through the cab and landed hard on the ground on the far side of the train.

"Keep yer filthy hands off me," the engineer said, grabbing a handle and pulling himself to his feet. "You was worse than the robbers."

"I saw one of them shoot your fireman."

"Well, yeah, there was that. The damned bakehead tried to save me and got hisself shot up." The engineer tried to look fierce but failed. "Reckon you done saved my life, too, even if you did try to kill me with all your slugs rattlin' 'round in the cab." He ran his finger over a bright silver smear where a slug had scraped along the iron wall.

"Anything damaged on the locomotive?"

"Everything's well built. Doesn't look like anything's busted. I kin git a head of steam up and get movin' inside fifteen, twenty minutes."

"Even with your busted wing?" Slocum pointed to the engineer's arm.

"I can highball jist fine long as there's someone to feed the firebox."

Marshal Lennox climbed back up, looking grim.

"They got away. The lot of them."

"We got here in time to keep the train from being robbed," Slocum said. "They might have killed more than they did."

"You fellas go find me someone able to shovel coal. I got a schedule to keep."

Slocum and Lennox dropped to the ground. Sonny Briggs and two of his posse came up. If Lennox had looked pissed at losing Stringfellow, Briggs was in a state of outright choler.

"We got four of them, but the rest got away. It's all your fault, Marshal. You should have waited for us."

"That would have been too late," Slocum cut in before Lennox could respond. "You took so long getting here, Stringfellow had already stopped the train and was killing off the train crew."

"He killed the fireman and conductor. Four passengers are all shot up." Briggs grunted. "We got to get after the gang 'fore they disappear into the mountains."

Slocum saw the posse laying out the dead. The conductor's uniform jacket was soaked with more blood than any man ought to have in his body. The fireman had been shot in the head. Three outlaws looked as if they had been used for target practice. Even from a distance, Slocum counted more than a dozen wounds on each of them. The posse had taken out their ire on the few outlaws they'd caught.

"The engineer needs someone to shovel coal for him. Any of the train crew able to do that?" Lennox asked.

"The mail clerk looked strong enough. A young kid but sturdy and he didn't get hit."

"Go fetch him. The engineer's champing at the bit to get steam up."

"It's important to keep to the schedule," Briggs said, as if reciting something the owner of the railroad had told him. He snapped back to the here and now. "We've got to get after them. You coming with us, Marshal?" He looked from Lennox to Slocum, relieved neither intended to join the railroad detectives. "No? You ride on into the depot with the train, then, while we run those rabid dogs to ground."

Briggs yelled orders. One of his men led his horse up. He swung into the saddle and the posse galloped away, silhouetted by the full sun. In less than a minute the dust from their horses settled and vanished, leaving only the fitful smoke puffing from the locomotive smoke stack.

"That the mail clerk?" Lennox asked when he saw a youngster plodding forward. "I've seen men climb up to the gallows faster than that."

"Ain't there anyone else who can do this?" The mail clerk looked at Lennox and the badge on his vest. "Might be you can deputize me to watch over the mail?"

"The engineer wants you to stoke," Slocum said. "Better get to it. He looks like a harsh taskmaster."

"Ben's a crazy old coot. Nobody likes him 'cuz—"

"Get yer cracker ass up here and shovel, damn you!" The engineer leaned out and motioned to the clerk. "We need steam to get movin'. Startin' up on a grade this steep is gonna take ever' bit of power this old rig can muster."

The mail clerk reluctantly grabbed a handrail and pulled himself up. He rolled up his sleeves and began shoveling while the engineer cursed, hammered at valves, and seated himself to tap the steam pressure gauge.

"From the look of it, the engine's been damaged," Slocum said. "See all the steam leaking out around the pistons?"

"Might have been a stray bullet or two," Lennox agreed. He looked around, then said, "Sonny and his men are long gone. It's time to get down to real work."

"What do you mean?" Slocum saw that the marshal had a secret eating him up inside.

"The gang lit out downhill when the railroad dicks joined the fight, but Stringfellow and that writer fellow went the other way. They rode out west. Stringfellow's the one I want."

Slocum kept his answer to himself as Melissa rode up, her eyes wide and her cheeks flushed.

"Did they capture them all?"

"They ran 'em off," Lennox said. "But me and Slocum are going after Stringfellow. You'd be best off trailing along after Sonny and his men."

"I'm not leaving you," Melissa said. Slocum wasn't sure if she meant the marshal or him. It didn't matter.

"We're goin' to be ridin' hard 'cuz I'm not lettin' String-fellow get away when he's this close."

"Or you can get on board the train," Slocum said. "Ride on into the depot. We'll get you there."

The train let out a long, loud whistle that spooked Melissa's horse. She fought to stay astride. The clanking and rattling followed by the sounds of wheels grinding down into the tracks were followed by the smell of hot metal.

"We're pullin' out," the engineer shouted. "All aboard what's gettin' aboard!"

"You should get aboard," Lennox said.

"I won't." Another whistle caused her horse to begin bucking.

Slocum exchanged a look with Lennox. Both of them mounted and galloped off, ahead of the train straining to build enough power to overcome the grade and the ponderous weight of the cars behind the engine.

"She'll follow us, you know," Lennox said. "That's not goin' to be good for any of us."

Slocum glanced over his shoulder. Melissa sat on the ground and her mount had run off, spooked by the ferocious noises from the iron horse.

"Unless she wants to walk, she's got to get aboard the train," Slocum said. He turned back and put his head down, keeping pace with the marshal.

They'd get Stringfellow this time. Stringfellow and his new partner, Rory Randolph.

14

"I don't see the trail." Slocum slowed and finally came to a complete stop so he could study the ground more closely. Nowhere did he see any hint of a horse riding across this stretch of rocky ground, much less a pair of horses. He looked up at Lennox and shook his head. "We've lost them."

"Like hell," growled Lennox. "I'm not giving up this easy." He swiveled about in the saddle, hunting for any sign of movement. The expression of disgust showed how futile the search was. "They can't get out of the hills like they're smoke blowin' on the wind."

Slocum didn't dispute the man's words, though he hardly thought of the towering peaks around them as hills. They were deep in the mountains. The day had started warm enough but now wind blew down off the upper reaches already covered in deep snow. If they found the outlaws soon, Slocum wouldn't freeze to death. Even with his light coat covered by his duster, he was beginning to feel the chill.

"They'll go to ground soon," he said. "They're no better equipped than we are. They'll want a fire to get warm."

"Where did they go? Stringfellow can't know these hills better 'n me."

Slocum saw the railroad tracks veering away to follow a branching canyon. Following his gut, Lennox had led them down another canyon, away from the train. Slocum's sense told him something entirely different.

"We need to follow the tracks."

"Why? They can get away if they ride north from here."

"They might not know that. They do know the tracks will take them out of the mountains and onto a prairie eventually."

Lennox thought on it a moment, then slowly agreed.

"There's a touch of truth to what you say, but if you're wrong, they're long past ever bein' caught."

"Same if you're wrong."

"We can split up," Lennox said.

Slocum remained silent. This was a bad idea. He let the marshal figure out why it was wrong for one of them to come upon two desperados.

"The tracks," Lennox finally said. "We follow them. It makes sense they'd ride along the railroad bed since they wouldn't leave obvious hoofprints in the ballast."

Slocum wheeled around and trotted off to reach the railroad tracks. He looked down the tracks and saw plumes of smoke coming from the locomotive stack.

"The train's moving slow. The damage must have been worse than you thought, Marshal. We're not too far behind it."

They couldn't push their tired horses faster than a brisk walk, but Slocum used the slow advance to keep a sharp eye out for the outlaws. It was getting dark and soon the best landmark Slocum had was the steam engine spewing out steam and embers into the air.

Lennox looked hard at him when a gunshot worked its way back from the train. Slocum urged his tired pinto forward, keeping up with the marshal for a hundred yards, then fell back slowly as his horse flagged. He saw the train stopped ahead. Foot-long muzzle flashes showed the fight beginning again. As hard as it was for Slocum to believe, Stringfellow hadn't given up trying to rob the train. His gang was scattered and being pursued by Briggs's posse, but he still had the balls to try the holdup a second time.

From ahead, Lennox's gun spat fire. The reply was immediate. The marshal kicked free of his horse and hit the ground running. He caught his toe and fell headlong. Even as far back as he rode, Slocum heard the air knocked out of the lawman's lungs. Whatever happened now, Lennox was a sitting duck unless Slocum diverted the outlaws' attention.

He did the best he could, riding to the far side of the train and firing toward the mail car. He came up on the side without the door so he kept riding until he reached the engine.

The engineer sat on the floor, holding his belly. He looked up forlornly.

"How bad you get shot this time, Ben?"

"Gut-shot me this time. Killed the young'un from the mail car. It was that wild-eyed one."

Slocum had faced Stringfellow and doubted there was ever a situation where the outlaw would become wild-eyed. That meant Rory Randolph had killed another man and shot the engineer while his new boss forced his way into the mail car.

"Can you get the train moving?"

The engineer nodded, then gasped out, "I'll need another stoker. We're losin' pressure something fierce, but I can keep the old girl movin' along at five, ten miles an hour. We're past the worst of the grades, and it's all level from here on."

"I'll see what I can do about finding you someone used to using a shovel," Slocum said. He dropped off his horse and worked his way between the coal tender and the first passenger car. He heard nothing but women crying and men cursing from inside. A quick look around the edge of the car convinced him he would be dead in an instant if he showed his face. Randolph stood guard outside the mail car four cars back, looking around. If there had been any doubt which of the train robbers was the wild-eyed one who had killed the mail clerk and shot Ben again, it was removed with that quick glance.

Slocum stepped up onto the metal steps and tried to open the door into the passenger car. Stuck. He braced himself and kicked hard. The door broke around something blocking it on the inside.

"You stay out! We're armed. We'll shoot if you try to come inside!"

"I'm riding with a posse. That's Marshal Lennox out there. I need to save him or we'll all be gunned down."

He shoved again and peered around the corner of the broken door. Three men and six women huddled together. One man held out his fist and waved it about.

"I got a derringer. You stay out!"

Slocum squeezed past and tumbled over the seats the passengers had used to block the door. He got to his feet and looked with disdain at the man with his fist thrust out.

"You've got a broken piece of metal. I told you I was with Marshal Lennox's posse. Have the robbers come through here?"

"I only seen two of 'em, but there's got to be more. We was robbed before, this morning. I knew somethin' was wrong when we limped along, barely movin' all day. Part of the time we was parked."

"Only the pair?" Slocum turned his cold eyes on the man to stop his nervous chatter.

The man clamped his mouth shut and nodded.

"Stay here. And put down that angle iron. You look dumb waving it around."

Slocum got a chuckle from one of the men and admiring looks from the women. He pushed past them and opened the door into the next passenger car. Whatever they had done to the door leading in proved beyond Slocum's strength to break. He climbed up to the roof of the car and made his way toward the mail car. When he got to the car just in front of it, he dropped to his belly.

It took him a few seconds to figure out what was happening. Two men in the mail car shot outside. The marshal had taken refuge in a shallow ditch alongside the tracks. The robbers couldn't get out but the marshal was also pinned down, and any attempt to stand or even retreat would mean his death.

Slocum waved to the marshal, hoping Lennox would recognize him in the dark. The lawman didn't try shooting him off the roof, so Slocum hoped this meant he had not only seen him in the darkness but identified him as a friend. If not, Slocum was about to get himself shot up from both sides.

He heard Stringfellow and Randolph moving around inside the car. He crawled to a spot just above the open door and waved to Lennox, hoping he understood what he was about to do. Then he drew his Colt Navy, took a breath, leaned over as far as he could, and poked his gun through the doorway. He opened fire. It was dark inside the mail car, and Slocum let instinct guide his aim. The outlaws screeched and dived for cover, but he got no sense that he had hit either of them.

"Come on out with your hands up," he shouted. "We won't gun you down, as much as you deserve it."

"That you, Slocum?"

"Melissa's going to be mighty disappointed in you, Randolph. She thought you were a law-abiding man."

Slocum ducked back as bullets tore through the car roof not an inch from his body. He rolled away and got to his feet, only to lose his balance when the train lurched and began moving. Struggling to stay on his feet, he took a couple quick steps toward the back of the train. The second step came down on empty air between cars. Flailing, he tumbled straight down, hitting his arm and losing his Colt as he fell. Moaning, Slocum forced himself to sit up.

He was staring down the barrel of Stringfellow's six-shooter.

"You are one slippery son of a buck," Stringfellow said. "Every time I think I got you dead to rights, you wiggle away. Not this time."

He straightened his arm and started to fire. The train lurched again and jiggled his aim. Slocum launched himself. He grabbed the outlaw's wrist and tried to slam it hard against the metal platform on the passenger car. It wouldn't give him an advantage, but it took away Stringfellow's superiority.

The train lurched again as if the engineer had finally built up enough steam power to get everything moving. Stringfellow and Slocum grappled, then the outlaw kicked out powerfully. Slocum winced as the boot toe crashed into his shin. Then Stringfellow surged upward and shoved hard, sending him tumbling backward. Slocum crashed back into the passenger car. Several passengers tried to help him up but only succeeded in holding him down.

"Let me up. He's getting away." Slocum lashed out and knocked away some of the well-meaning men. He stumbled back to the platform and saw the end of the mail car growing smaller.

A quick look down confirmed his suspicion. Stringfellow had uncoupled the mail car. Slocum dropped to his knees, found his six-gun, and then jumped from the moving train. He hit the ground and rolled. When he got his feet under him, Marshal Lennox was already at his side.

"They got away, Slocum. Stringfellow uncoupled the cars, letting the passenger cars go."

"But the mail car and caboose. They're not going anywhere. He uncoupled them and—"

Slocum saw that the train chugged onward, leaving behind the last two cars. Nowhere did he see Stringfellow or Randolph.

"They got to their horses in the confusion," Lennox said. "I don't see so good at night. They mighta took advantage of me that way. I heard them ridin' off, though. They went back in the direction of the branching canyon."

"Did they steal anything?"

Lennox started to speak, then clamped his mouth shut and scowled.

"That never occurred to me to find out."

Slocum jumped up into the mail car. Sacks of mail were strewn all over. More than one had stopped a bullet during the fight. He went to the safe and saw the door standing wide open. With a quick movement, he got out a lucifer and flicked it to life. The brief flare died and gave flickering light. A few greenbacks were left behind as mute reminder of how many had been in the safe before the robbery.

"They got a whale of a lot of money, is my guess," Lennox said. He pointed to a large stack of loose mail. "They ripped open the canvas mailbag and used it to carry off the money from the safe."

"How'd they get it open so slick? They had to know the combination. Otherwise, it would take a couple sticks of dynamite to blow the door off." Slocum ran his fingers over the edge of the thick steel door. He didn't even find any nicks to show they had tried to pry it open.

"It can only mean Stringfellow had the combination."

They stared at each other, then said simultaneously, "The mail clerk."

"Reckon he was an inside man," Lennox said. "That might be why he was shot down like he was, to keep him from spilling his guts."

Slocum had to disagree. "It'd be better for Stringfellow to have a fall guy."

"So why'd they shoot him?"

"*They* didn't kill him," Slocum said. "Rory Randolph did."

"That writer fellow's gone plumb loco. Was he fixin' to ride with Stringfellow from the start? Is he even a writer? All we know is what Miss Benton told us."

"He's a writer," Slocum said, remembering how Stringfellow had dropped the damning dime novel and then ripped up another Randolph had written with him as the dastardly villain. "No telling what's going through his head. He might be doing this, thinking he's researching another book."

"From the men he's killed that we know about, he's not going to research anything but dancin' at the end of a rope."

"Trailing them in the dark is going to be hard," Slocum said. "We'd better get to it."

"First chore's goin' to be findin' our horses. They run off when the shootin' started." Lennox hitched up his gun belt, turned his collar to the wind, and started climbing the rung ladder on the end of the mail car.

Slocum stepped away and waited for the marshal to spot his horse. In the dark it wouldn't be easy, but from atop the car it had to be easier. And it was. When Lennox pointed, Slocum started walking. He found the marshal's horse cropping at what remained of some grass. He caught the reins and led the horse back.

Lennox climbed down from the mail car, settled himself in the saddle, then reached down to help Slocum up behind him.

"Your horse is a quarter mile off. Might be more by the time we get there."

Slocum spotted his pinto before the marshal, dismounted, and spent a few minutes gentling the horse. The pinto hardly balked when he stepped up. He tried to remember when he had spent as much time in the saddle as out. Even on the roundup, he had only worked four-hour shifts.

"If we follow the tracks back to the branch in the canyons, we'll be taking the same trail as those two owlhoots," Lennox said. "I'd cut across country, but the tracks are about as straight a path as we're goin' to find."

"How much did they make off with?" Slocum asked.

"Enough so they'll want to run their horses into the ground to get away. From everything I heard and what Sonny said, the shipment might be as much as a thousand dollars."

"Split two ways, that's a real good day's work," Slocum said. He wondered if Stringfellow would bother splitting the money with Randolph. Better to get behind the writer and shoot him in the back. That doubled his take for the price of a single cartridge.

"More 'n either of us will see this year. Even if the town fathers decided to give me a raise, I wouldn't see anywhere near that much."

They rode, conversation slowly falling into longer silences until they came to the vee in the canyons.

"That canyon goes north to a road into Canada. If Stringfellow has got any sense, that's where he'll head. Idaho is gettin' too hot for him with the railroad bulls comin' out in force."

"And you," Slocum said. "Having a big town marshal after you isn't something to brag about." He sniffed the air and smiled. He had found the outlaws.

"I caught a whiff of the campfire, too. Smells like they burned their beans." Lennox checked his six-gun and then slid it back into his holster. "I wish I hadn't lost my rifle. When they had me pinned down, I needed to do some fancy runnin'. The rifle got lost in the dark."

"Want to use mine?"

"You keep it. My handgun will do me just fine."

"They camped behind that rise," Slocum said. "We dismount here, sneak up, and get the drop on them."

"And have them in Idaho Falls by day after tomorrow. I like the way you think, Slocum."

The two dismounted and tied up their horses before advancing on the outlaws' camp. They crept over the top, warily trying to find their quarry in the camp below. Slocum made out a bedroll, but something warned him.

"They're not—"

That's all the farther he got before he heard the telltale metallic click of a six-shooter cocking behind him.

"Grab a piece of heaven, why don't you?"

Slocum did as he was told, turned slowly, and stared down the barrel of Rory Randolph's six-gun. Beside him, he heard Lennox suck in a deep breath and hold it. Then he let it out slowly.

"Lennox, don't," Slocum warned.

But the marshal wasn't going to be taken prisoner. He whirled about, his hand flashing to his pistol. The still night was ripped apart by the report from Randolph's gun. Slocum was dazzled by the muzzle flash. He blinked away the dancing yellow and blue spots and saw the marshal on the ground.

"Your aim's gotten too good," Slocum said. "You shot Marshal Lennox square in the heart. What are you going to do about me?"

Slocum tensed when he heard Stringfellow say from the dark, "Go on, Randolph. Cut him down, too. Show him you're a real man."

Randolph cocked his pistol again and aimed it straight at Slocum's head.

15

"I don't cotton much to lawmen. Lennox dying doesn't mean a whole lot to me," Slocum said. He felt sweat beading on his forehead. The wind swept it away and turned his flesh to ice. He worked to keep any hint of fear from his voice, but he knew he was in a pickle that would end badly for him, no matter what. "I've ridden with more than one gang of train robbers in my day. You pulled off that heist slick as shit on ice."

"You think so? It was my idea. Will wanted to quit and ride off when the posse shot us up back at the pass, but I convinced him to try once more."

"A thousand dollars," Slocum said. "That what you took? That's a powerful lot of money. More 'n you could make as a writer."

He saw the way Randolph tensed. He had touched a nerve and had to figure out how to smooth ruffled feathers or die.

"Is that one of your plots? Missing your chance at one robbery, then trying again and succeeding?"

"My plots," Randolph snarled. "Is that what the bitch told you? Is that what Melissa claims?"

142

"You don't have to be under her thumb out here. But you don't have to be under Stringfellow's either. You're smart."

"Damned right I am. And I'm not under Will's thumb. We're partners. Isn't that right, Will?"

Struggling up the hill came the outlaw. He clutched his right arm. Thick black drops of blood oozed over his fingers and dripped to the ground. Lennox must have winged him, but the wound didn't take him out of the fight. He couldn't hold a gun in his shooting hand, but his words were as deadly.

"Don't fool around with him, Randolph. Just shoot him. I would but you see how I'm all shot up. Kill him. You did in the marshal. What's the difference with this snake in the grass?"

"Him and Melissa, they spent time together."

"She doesn't mean anything to me, Rory," Slocum said, seeing the problem more clearly now. "All she said was how much she wanted you. She even called out your name when we were—"

"Shut up!" Randolph screeched like an owl and clapped his left hand to his ear. If his right clutching his six-shooter had wavered a fraction of an inch, Slocum would have tested his luck and thrown down on him. "It wasn't like that. I know it wasn't. I've wanted her from the first day I saw her at Five Points."

"Five Points?"

"In New York. There she was all hoity-toity and uppity, strutting along like she owned the cobblestones under her expensive shoes. I saved her from a couple Whyos wanting to rob her, maybe rape her for good measure."

"Whyos?" Slocum played for time. If Randolph talked, he wasn't shooting. And Stringfellow dared not interrupt his newfound partner. The writer was too mercurial to trust with a gun.

"They joined up with the Chichesters and they both wiped out the Dead Rabbits." Randolph shook his head as if something rattled inside. "Gangs. From the waterfront. Five Points. I saved her hide, and the bitch wouldn't ever put out for me. You show up and she can't hike her skirts fast enough."

"You and her are a team," Slocum said. "That's something better than sex."

"No, it's not! You don't know how she torments me!"

"Randolph, just get on with it. Shoot the bastard. The rest of the posse must be around somewhere if this one and the marshal found us." Stringfellow came over. Not only did he clutch his right arm, but his right leg dragged a mite. Slocum realized how shot up the outlaw was. In any kind of a fight now, he was a loser.

"A thousand dollars split two ways isn't as good as keeping it all for yourself," Slocum said.

"He's trying to turn you against me. Hell, man, shoot him!" Stringfellow coughed and spat blood. "We got to ride. I warned you they'd be on our trail. I was right. Now I'm telling you the rest of the posse, all them railroad bulls, won't rest until they find us."

"Will can keep the money. All of it," Randolph said. A sneer crossed his lips. "He's given me a chance to show what I can do."

"You were a gang member in New York," Slocum said. "Killing's not going to keep you awake at night."

"I never used a gun before. I like six-shooters. Back in New York I always used a slungshot. I'd creep up behind and bash in their skulls 'fore I robbed 'em. The cops came down like a load of bricks if they caught any of us with a gun. They don't care about saps or clubs. Most of my gang carried knives, but I liked the feel of a man's head crushing to bloody pulp when I hit him."

Slocum cast a quick look at Stringfellow. The outlaw's eyes went wide in surprise. This wasn't what he'd expected from a man who spent his days with a pen in hand writing about violence. Not a trace of lie came with Randolph's spilled memories. Somehow Melissa had harnessed his anger and brutality and channeled it into the dime novels.

"That must be the same feeling you had when you wrote all that about Stringfellow and what he did to his ma and sister." Slocum prodded the outlaw to act. Even if he couldn't use his six-gun or punch out the writer, any distraction gave the chance for shooting it out.

"Randolph, listen to me. He's trying to turn you against me. I gave you the chance to ride with me. I wasn't wrong. You're as good as any who's ever been in my gang. I forgive you all those lies. It was as you said. Just fiction. Potboilers to give the rubes a thrill or two."

"Only he wasn't lying. He knew you did those things," Slocum said to stir the pot as much as he could.

"Will's right. It's time for you to die, Slocum."

Slocum feinted left and dived right. At the same time he went for his Colt. The slug's impact knocked him spinning. He landed hard and began rolling downhill. Randolph kept firing, but the moving target eluded him now. When he reached the bottom of the hill, Slocum tried to stand, only to have his foot slide out from under him. One of Randolph's slugs had shot off his boot heel.

Flopping forward on the ground, he brought his Colt to bear. For a brief instant, one of the men silhouetted himself against the starry sky. Slocum fired. Even as his finger came back on the trigger, he knew it was an impossible shot. He missed by a country mile.

"I'm coming for you, Slocum. You and Melissa aren't ever going to spend another night together. You can't know how I wanted her for my own."

"Take her, dammit," called Slocum. "She doesn't mean anything to me."

"That's why I have to kill you. You had her, and she's not worth scraping off your boots."

Slocum heard Stringfellow yammering. Randolph was beyond reason. Trying to stay alive, Slocum had pushed the writer over the edge of sanity.

He braced his pistol on the ground, aimed toward the top

of the rise, and waited for his chance. Slocum flinched when a rifle shot ripped through the night. Then he looked around. Both horses Stringfellow and Randolph had ridden were on the far side of their camp. He thought he made out the shadowy rifle stocks still riding in saddle sheaths.

A dull crack from a handgun was immediately answered by several rifle shots. This caused confused argument between Randolph and Stringfellow. Then there was only silence.

Slocum had to keep the outlaws on the defensive. He got his feet under him, braced for an uneven gait because of the missing heel, then charged uphill, firing as he went.

"We got 'em, men. Get the posse to box 'em in!" Slocum's throat turned raw from shouting everything he could think of to give the impression that Sonny Briggs and his posse had joined the battle.

As he stumbled to the crest, he fleetingly thought he hadn't been lying. More rifle fire from the direction of the railroad tracks made him hope that Briggs and his men had found him. He dropped to his knees and fumbled to reload. Slocum worked faster when he saw a dark figure coming toward him. He only got two cartridges in before lifting the pistol to fire. Better two shots than none.

A hand knocked the pistol off target and then grabbed his wrist.

"We must go." The harsh command shocked him. He looked up into Lost Horse's eyes.

"You have my pinto?"

"This way." The Cree brave darted into the darkness, leaving behind the confused ravings of Stringfellow and Randolph.

Slocum wanted to put an end to their crime spree but wanted to save his own life more. After two steps he knew he couldn't walk well with a missing heel. But the few seconds of being slower cost him. He had lost the Indian but kept stumbling along in the dark until he saw his pinto standing patiently, waiting for him. Grabbing the saddle horn, he pulled himself up and only then did he look around.

Lost Horse approached, already mounted. He held the rifle high and fired it, then let out a war whoop. He looked sheepish as he lowered it and said, "No harm in scaring them more."

"I want them," Slocum said. "I want both of them. Get your party together, and we can cut them off before they get to their horses." He sank back in the saddle when he realized that he was looking at the entire rescue party.

"You want revenge. What is there for me?"

"Their horses and blankets." He let out a deep sigh. "You can have the marshal's horse and tack, too."

"Already mine," Lost Horse said proudly. Then he stared at Slocum with eyes that defied reading. "He was your friend?"

"As close as I have until you pulled my fat from the fire."

"We are not blood brothers."

"Friends don't have to be, but you are strong and a skilled warrior. I would be honored if you were my blood brother."

Lost Horse turned away, deep in thought. Slocum knew better than to disturb him. He took the time to reload from ammo he carried in his saddlebags. He had been through a small war this day alone. When the shooting stopped, his gun had to be cleaned and oiled. It was a precision instrument of death and had served him well over the years. Keeping it in tiptop working condition would keep him alive over even more years.

But now it was time to put a few more rounds through its barrel.

"You will fight me for the horse?"

"No," Slocum said. "I give my friend's horse to you as a gift. It is my way of showing we are friends."

"Friends," scoffed the Indian. "That is the word the Canadians used before they drove us from our land."

"That's the word the Great White Father uses to drive other tribes from their land," Slocum said. "It is not a word I use as lightly."

"I can have the others' horses?"

"And tack. And rifles."

"They ride north in this canyon. Catching them will be hard in the dark."

"I am sure Lost Horse is a great tracker. You have eyes like an owl and the speed of a striking snake."

"True," the Indian admitted immodestly, "but they have a great start."

Slocum tugged on the reins and got his horse moving toward Stringfellow's camp. He saw how they had laid the trap, putting out blankets with rocks and brush piled underneath to gull an unsuspecting scout into thinking they slept. The pair had left the dummies in place, but their horses were gone.

"They robbed a train of a thousand dollars," Slocum said. He dropped from the saddle and poked around in the camp. A few extra minutes mattered little, and he might find something worthwhile. All he found was his boot heel.

He sat by the fire and positioned it. The nails remained in spite of a huge nick shot from the side. He positioned it on his boot, then used a rock to hammer it back into place. A few tentative steps convinced him it would stay in place until he got a cobbler to properly attach it. If he didn't have to hike far, it would serve him well enough.

"Do they have more than white man's paper money?"

"From the look of the camp, they lit out and left most of their supplies," Slocum said. He took what he wanted and gave the rest to Lost Horse.

Only then did he mount and trot along to catch up. He and Lost Horse rode side by side for more than an hour without finding any trace of the outlaw and the writer.

"Is there a trail to the canyon rim?" Slocum asked. "If Stringfellow got antsy about being trailed, he would try to get out of here."

"No trail for horses. On foot only," Lost Horse said.

Slocum hadn't seen any abandoned horses. From the quick glimpse he had of the outlaw, Stringfellow's injuries

kept him from hoofing it all the way to the canyon rim a
hundred feet above them. He rode or he died. That thought
turned Slocum cautious, and he began jumping at shadows
so much that Lost Horse drew rein and leaned to whisper,
"You fear them. Do not. We will kill them!"

"I'm not afraid of them," Slocum said. "I know they can't
ride much further. Leastways, Stringfellow can't with those
wounds."

"Would he lay a trap while the other rides away?"

"Maybe," Slocum said, thinking hard. He was more convinced that Randolph would leave Stringfellow behind, in
spite of the way the writer had attached himself to the outlaw. It was almost as if he needed someone telling him what
to do and how to behave. When he went out on his own, he
turned violent and crazy.

"They are tired. They cannot ride all night," Lost Horse
said.

"That means they're fixing up an ambush for us," Slocum
said. He turned this over in his head. It worked to his advantage. If the two kept riding, he and Lost Horse would never
overtake them.

But what if they couldn't keep riding? Stringfellow's injuries
might hamper them. Or their horses were tuckered out. Slocum
felt his own sturdy pinto falter now and again. It had been ridden almost into the ground. A lesser horse might be ready to
give up the ghost at any turn. An ambush became more likely.

"If they stop, we have them," Slocum said. "The canyon's
wide. You ride along the far wall, and I'll hug this one."

Lost Horse understood and veered away without another
word. By separating, only one of them would ride into any
ambush. That gave the other the chance to come to his partner's aid.

As Slocum thought on that, he grinned. It had been a while
since he had ridden the trail with anyone he considered a
partner. The whole time spent wrangling, he had been friendly
with the other drovers but none had been worth calling a

partner. Marshal Lennox had come close. They'd been bound together with a desire to see Stringfellow stopped, but the lawman had fallen now. This added to the reasons Slocum wanted to put a bullet into the outlaw's belly, but seeing him hang for murdering the marshal would be good enough.

He slowed and then came to a halt when he heard movement ahead. At this time of night, most predators were in their burrows sleeping because their prey was also sleeping. Owls and other night birds might go after incautious vermin, but such game was sparse out here. Rabbits and larger game fed only at dusk and dawn, preferring to stay safe from wolves, coyotes, and mountain lions whenever possible.

Whatever moved ahead was intended to distract him. Slocum dismounted and slapped the pinto's rump, sending it trotting toward the sound.

Slocum was glad he was so foresighted. Stringfellow moved from hiding nearby and hefted a rifle clumsily. His right arm had been bandaged in such a way that he could curl his finger around the trigger. How he held the rifle was hidden from Slocum by the man's body.

Stringfellow wasn't the threat. Randolph was. The best the outlaw could do was fire once. Levering in a new round was out of the question with his arm all tied up the way it was. Slocum bided his time and was glad he did. Randolph came from the underbrush. Slocum had not spotted him.

"Where'd the varmint go? He's not on the horse."

"He knows it's a trap. Get back, you idiot, get back!" Stringfellow fired off his one round and awkwardly returned to his hiding spot. It might take him a minute or longer to load a new round.

Slocum took careful aim and squeezed off a round in Randolph's direction. The man yelped like a scalded dog and ducked back into the brush. Slocum filled the area with rounds until his Colt came up empty. He began reloading.

"I see him, Rory. He's back along the trail. He used his horse to decoy us out."

Slocum bided his time, waiting for a good shot. Instead, Lost Horse ruined his waiting game by riding up and presenting a decent target behind him.

Stringfellow got off another shot that caused the Indian's horse to rear. The Cree might as well have been glued to its back. He held on and brought the frightened horse under control.

"Stringfellow's got a rifle. I'm going after Randolph."

Slocum lit out running. In the dark he was a difficult target, but no one shot at him. He zigzagged and finally came to the clump of brush where Randolph had taken cover. Nothing. He poked around, hunting for a trail, and came up empty-handed. Giving up wasn't in his nature, but he had no spoor to follow, no hint where the writer had gone other than farther along the canyon.

Lost Horse rode up with the pinto's reins in his hand.

Slocum mounted, a cold fury building in him.

"We came close. They can't be more than a few minutes ahead."

"There are many canyons. Caves. If they hide, we will never find them. If they split up, do we?"

Slocum winced as he moved. His right side was soaked in blood. He had been wounded and never noticed until now.

"I won't give up."

"I return to my tribe's campfire." Lost Horse wheeled about and rode back the way they had come.

Slocum hesitated, considering what lay ahead—or what didn't. Finding Stringfellow and Randolph would be harder than ever now. The best chance of catching them had been turning the tables at the ambush. With that opportunity gone, Slocum faced endless hours of hunting for a trail that might not exist.

He turned his pinto and trotted after Lost Horse. Having the Cree medicine man patch him up became more important with every mile he rode as the bullet wound's ache turned to outright pain.

16

Slocum awoke with a start. For a second he wasn't sure where he was. Strange odors made his nostrils flare and caused him to choke. He rolled onto his side and winced at the pain. He carefully moved so he was flat on his back. Taking shallow breaths helped. Only when the pain subsided did he blink hard. Tears washed the smoke from his eyes, and he saw a curious conical roof.

"Tipi," he said. Everything rushed back.

He and Lost Horse had found the Cree campground. It was only a day before, but from the way he had awakened, he might have been drugged. Gently moving his fingers over his side, he traced out the wound. The bullet had cut deeper than he had thought. The ride back had opened the hole in his side and caused him the pain.

"Rib," came a distant explanation. "The bullet rode along your rib."

He propped himself on his elbows. Lost Horse sat cross-legged at the tipi entrance, smoking a pipe. He held it out for Slocum. Moving gingerly, Slocum sat up. The pain faded like an echo. He scooted over and took the pipe. Sharing

152

tobacco like this was a ritual and demanded his full attention. A lung filled with the smoke threatened to make him cough, but he fought back the reflex. Lost Horse nodded solemnly.

"Good. Medicine man worried you had a hole inside that would leak smoke."

Slocum laughed and immediately regretted it.

"You expected the smoke to come out my ears?"

"Your side." Lost Horse pointed with the pipe. "You hurt but this will go quickly. The bone was not broken."

Slocum traced over his side and winced again, but he found nothing to contradict Lost Horse or, more likely, the Cree medicine man. Patiently, he waited for Lost Horse to take another appreciative puff, look at the pipe, and then pass it back. This time the smoke soothed Slocum and relaxed his tight muscles. By the time the bowl held only ash, he felt almost human.

"It's a good thing you talked me into returning to your camp," Slocum said. "If I'd gone after those two owlhoots, I'd've probably passed out and died."

"Our hunting parties seek them. They rode north, then cut east and possibly return to your settlement."

"Idaho Falls?"

Lost Horse nodded. He tapped out the bowl and ceremoniously put it into a deerskin sheath. Slocum had a chance to look around and realized this was the medicine man's tipi. Pouches of herbs were scattered about, possibly at random, but he doubted that. Some kept away bad spirits. Others added to the thick scent inside the tent.

"How long have I been passed out?"

"Days. Three, four."

"Plenty of time for Stringfellow and Randolph to get away," Slocum said glumly.

"You will not give up hunting them. You can go to the white man's town and ask for them."

"They went there because there's no law to stop them.

Randolph killed the marshal, and Lennox didn't have a deputy that I know of. Briggs and his railroad detectives went after the others in the gang. By now they are scattered all over the Northwest."

"Would they not hire a new lawman?"

"The mayor or whoever runs the town has to know Lennox is dead. I'm the only one who can take the news back to Idaho Falls. You can bet your bottom dollar neither Randolph nor Stringfellow will tell them."

Even as the words left his mouth, Slocum wondered how true that was. Randolph had tasted blood and liked it. Boasting of his murders might go a ways toward feeding his need for attention. A writer lived by being noticed. Randolph had killed and now wanted to be notorious like Stringfellow. From what the writer had said, he might have killed before back in New York, but the feel had to be different now.

Slocum had killed in so many ways. During the war he had been a sniper. Perched in a tree all day waiting for the flash of sunlight off an officer's braid had developed his patience. After the single killing shot, he always retreated. The shot, the death, they were mixed up together with one being identical to the other. He fired his rifle. Someone died. The death was diminished.

After he had ridden west, he had used a knife and his bare hands and firearms to defend himself and, often enough so that he wasn't too proud of it, simply to survive by robbery. After the war, he had never taken money to kill a man and never would, but the opportunities for death stretched endlessly on the frontier. How Rory Randolph had found this out was something of a puzzle to him, but the solution to the problem wasn't. He reached for his left side, where his Colt usually hung.

"Yours is a fine gun," Lost Horse said.

Slocum thought a moment and finally said, "You are my brother. It is yours."

"You are my brother. I give it back to you as a gift."

Slocum got to his feet and walked around. His legs wobbled but strengthened as he moved. He had settled his standing with the Cree. If Lost Horse considered him a brother, the others would also. And he would have his six-shooter where it belonged when he needed it.

"There is no trace of the two?"

"Hunters have seen the men who seek them."

"Sonny Briggs and his men," Slocum said. "Did they capture many of Stringfellow's gang?"

"Only two." Lost Horse pursed his lips, then added, "They were hung and left for the animals."

"That leaves Stringfellow with two or three men, depending on how I want to count Randolph. He can cause quite a bit of mischief with a gang that size."

But would he? The train robbery had given him more money than most robbers saw in a year of stickups. A thousand dollars would put a man up in style for quite a while. Even if Stringfellow split it with Randolph, that was a powerful lot of money. Why continue robbing, especially considering how shot up Stringfellow was?

"The gang might be out of the territory by now, with or without Stringfellow," Slocum went on. "I owe it to Lennox to get Randolph, but Stringfellow and the rest? I'm not a lawman, and I won't spend the rest of my life hunting them down."

"Would you hunt for this Randolph?"

Slocum tried to find an answer that satisfied him and Lost Horse, but nothing came. He had to think more on it. Another thought cropped up, though.

"Where is the woman? She wasn't on the train. If she had been, she would have gotten in the way when the marshal and I were shooting it out with Stringfellow and Randolph. Was she with Briggs and his men?"

"No one has seen her," Lost Horse said.

Slocum pressed his hand into his ribs. They still hurt like hell, but he knew he had to get in the saddle soon and find

Melissa. The steam whistle had spooked her horse and
thrown her. She hadn't been hurt by the fall, but she hadn't
gotten on the train, and running down a frightened horse
might have been too much for her. She was out in the mountains. If she had tried to find Randolph, she was either wandering around aimlessly or dead.

Slocum left the Cree camp the next morning to find her.

He rode up and down the length of tracks on the grade leading to the middle of the pass. He saw blood spattered on
rocks where men had bled out. Spent brass cartridges from
both pistols and rifles littered the area. In time their sheen
would weather and fade, but now they cast back rays of sun
that almost blinded him. He forced himself to look away
from the ground and at the surrounding terrain. Melissa's
horse had run downhill. He slowly made his way down the
incline, keen eyes not missing a turned rock or a broken
twig on a bush. In less than five minutes he left behind the
scene where the robbery had occurred.

The tracks stretched as straight as an arrow toward the
flat leading up to this pass. If the woman had any sense, she
would have caught her horse and followed the tracks to a
way station. If she hadn't been able to recover her horse,
doing anything but staying close to the tracks made no sense.

But then, not much of what Melissa Benton did made a
whale of a lot of sense to him. He stopped and looked at a patch
of earth that had been cut up by horses' hooves. Spiraling out,
he found only a single set left from here. The trail he followed
might belong to an outlaw, but evidence from other spots
showed where Briggs and his men had pursued a few riders.

This was a solitary trail. It would end with him finding
Melissa or another of the outlaws. As he rode, it increasingly
meant little to him which it was. By midafternoon he perked
up when he saw a scrap of cloth caught on a thorn bush. He
turned up his collar against the increasingly brisk wind and
looked up to the highest mountain peaks. Leaden clouds

gathered and threatened a storm. Bending low, he caught at the cloth and held it up.

It had come from Melissa's skirt. This was her trail. He rode faster now and found horse flop along a game trail winding higher into the hills. The wind in his face brought tears to his eyes and forced him to tie his bandanna over his nose to keep from sucking in frigid air. His side still ached, but he ignored this when he saw a horse cropping at what grass remained amid a small field.

He approached carefully, not wanting to spook the animal. It still carried a saddle and supplies lashed on behind. Edging closer, he finally grabbed for the reins. The horse tried to bolt and run, but he held it securely until it settled down. Only then did he give it some rein and let it walk about. When it picked out a direction across the field, he gave it its head and followed behind.

Melissa lay on the ground, not moving. He secured both horses and went to her, raising her head. Her eyelids flickered, but she didn't open her eyes. Chapped lips tried to form words but failed. Slocum picked her up and winced as the pain jabbed into his ribs, as if he had been stabbed. Carrying her to a spot amid some rocks to help protect her from the wind, he laid her down, then brought their horses over. If a storm blew through, this wasn't much shelter, but he wasn't up for cutting limbs from trees and making a lean-to.

As it was, he was giddy from the pain in his side after gathering wood and starting a fire. When the fire brought some blood back to the woman's cheeks, he set about boiling water and making oatmeal. He doubted she could get down much more than this.

Night came after he had finished feeding her. With darkness came a small snow flurry. Slocum propped up his duster like a tent against the wind and huddled down near the fire with Melissa in his arms. She was as cold as a corpse but stirred more now. He occasionally wetted her lips and gave her whatever she could take to drink.

By the time the storm blew full force, Slocum had her wrapped up in a blanket and stretched beside her by the fire. Their shared warmth brought more life to her, and she began thrashing about. Wrapped in the blanket as she was prevented her from flopping into the fire, but she started groaning and mumbling.

"Damn you, Rory, don't do this. You ungrateful wretch . . ."

Slocum listened to her nightmare, and sometime around midnight her eyes flickered open. She focused on his face only inches away and plainly said, "You're not Rory. John?"

"Rest," he said. "Your horse threw you."

"I hear wind. And it's cold, so cold."

"When the storm blows over, we'll head back to Idaho Falls."

"Don't want to go back, not until I find that ingrate. Rory owes me, and he's going to pay!"

"Don't waste your energy."

"I'll rip his tongue out. I'll pull his fingernails out with pliers. That'll show him, after all I've done for him. He can't run off like this."

"You and him weren't sleeping together," Slocum said, remembering what Randolph had said. "Why get so upset?"

"I made him what he was. He was nothing, nothing!"

"He was only a lowlife from Five Points," Slocum said.

"A street thug, good for nothing but petty robberies. He can't run off like this. He's shooting people. After all I've done for him, he's gone back to doing what he promised he'd left behind, back in New York, back with the gangs."

She wore herself out bad-mouthing Randolph. Slocum let her run down and held her the entire while. She hadn't been coherent, and that made Slocum wonder how much of what she said was true. Randolph was the writer, but Melissa sounded as if she had turned him into the one made famous by the dime novels.

The wind whistled and caused his duster to flap about. He made certain it was securely fastened, checked the horses as they stood rumps into the wind and heads down, then returned. Melissa had curled into a tight ball. He made sure the blanket covered her, then settled down himself with his saddle as a pillow. When he rolled over to get more comfortable, he saw her saddlebags.

On impulse, he opened them and fished about until he found the pad of paper she constantly wrote on. Holding it up to the firelight, he slowly read what she had written.

Her cramped, tight cursive proved hard for him to follow, but he had nothing better to do. He hesitated to sleep and let the fire die down too much with the snow flurry threatening to freeze them both before morning. He thought he had plenty of wood stacked against a lengthy storm, but if he had to, the paper would keep the fire going another few minutes.

He read and slowly became engrossed in what Melissa had written.

He looked over at her and understood why she was so mad at Rory Randolph. She had made him what he was. He was the acknowledged writer, but from the description Slocum read of the train robbery, Melissa was the author, not Randolph. He was the public face, the novelist who attended parties and made the social rounds with her at his side, but she wrote the books that made him famous.

From what he read, she had started another potboiler filled with gunfights and vicious outlaws killing and raping at will. And she had written in a hero who stood up against it all with unswerving bravery.

Slocum decided he liked his role in her novel better than Will Stringfellow ever could his as a mother-killer and sister-rapist. Still, he put the pad down and stared at it. All it would take was a quick flick of his wrist to send the sheets into the fire and consign them to oblivion.

He thought about it so long, he drifted off to sleep with the pad held down by his hand.

17

Slocum snapped fully awake when he felt the pad of paper slipping under his hand. He pressed down hard and stopped Melissa from taking it.

"That's mine," she said. Her lovely face was reddened, chapped by the wind and weather, and her voice came out as a croak more fitting for a frog. "You can't look at it."

"I already did," Slocum said.

He released the paper. She grabbed it and held it to her breast as if it were a small child. She glared at him, then worked to tuck it away safely in her saddlebags. Only when it was secure did she look at him.

"What are you going to do about it?"

"Do?" This startled Slocum. "I don't understand."

"You know who's really writing the books. Are you going to tell the newspapers and expose me as a fraud?"

"Looks to me as if Randolph is the fraud. He's claiming to be the writer and that you're nothing but a secretary. Is he blackmailing you?"

"Of course not. He's nothing. A no-account snake in the grass. He's not worth the time it would take to kick his butt out into the . . . into the snow." She stared past Slocum at the freshly fallen white ground cover. Almost an inch had fallen during the night as a prelude to real storms later in the winter. "He's beneath my contempt."

"Why is he claiming to be the writer?"

"Isn't it obvious? I'm a woman. Women can't write that kind of—" She swallowed hard and rubbed at her eyes. Tears leaked out. She sat straighter with a dignity Slocum doubted possible for one so disheveled. "That kind of fiction. No one can believe a woman writes that, but I do. I do it well, but when an author becomes popular, society demands appearances."

"You hired Randolph to go to these appearances?" Slocum laughed. "He's an ugly wart on a hog's ass compared to you."

"Thank you, if that was a compliment."

"It was," Slocum said. "You hired him and then tagged along to bask in the glory."

"Adulation pours out for my work. It would vanish if anyone learned a mere woman wrote it. I found Rory when he was a gang member."

"At Five Points. He saved you from being robbed."

Melissa harumphed and wrinkled her nose as if she had smelled something rotten.

"He would say that. I intervened with the police when he was arrested for robbing an old woman. If he said it was at Five Points, that's where it was. I don't remember. I was slumming, looking for story ideas. In that part of town, they pop from doorways and crawl down the streets onto a real author's page."

"He's moved up to killing anyone in front of his gun," Slocum said.

"Rory is a terrible person. I should have known I could never polish a turd."

"What are you going to do when Randolph gets a wanted poster put out for him?"

"I haven't thought of that. The best that can happen is for him to get killed, shot during a robbery. I can work that into a book and make him a hero, no matter what terrible thing he was doing."

Slocum marveled at how she went from hating the man for betraying her to making him a hero, just to preserve her writing.

"You'll have to find someone else to be the public author. Either that or you'll have to fess up and claim yourself as author."

"I could always claim Rory held me captive." She shook her head. "That won't work. I tried for years to sell my work, but the publishers never believed a woman could write about the West."

Slocum saw no reason to agree with those publishers. The bullshit she passed off in her potboilers had nothing to do with the actual life out West. He might have gotten into gunfights, but they were seconds of stark fear and sudden death compared to long hours in the saddle herding cattle. The reason he drank when he went into town was to kill the pain from the harsh conditions and hard work. Out with a herd, he never drank. None of the wranglers did. It was too easy to get killed by a cow making a sudden turn with a set of horns capable of driving through a thick wood plank. Fall off a horse and get trampled. Or kicked. Or simply make a bad decision and end up dead in some of the most beautiful and inhospitable country in the world.

"Well," Melissa said, "I need to find a solution to that problem, but I will." Her determination came through loud and strong. "First, Stringfellow and his gang have to be brought to justice."

"For your book?"

He saw that was mostly her reason for such a declaration. She let the real outlaw dictate the plot, only Stringfellow had committed a crime worse than robbery or murder. He had stolen away her puppet, and now she had to work around Randolph's treachery.

"I tried to follow the posse but got lost. They traveled so fast. Did they catch Stringfellow?"

"They went after his gang," Slocum said. He told her how the outlaw and her fake author had robbed the train and escaped after gunning down the marshal.

"I need a finale for the book. Stringfellow has to be brought to justice."

"He's all shot up and might not be in charge."

"Are you saying Rory might be leading the gang? Absurd. He's a follower, not a leader."

"They'd have to tie up somewhere for the gang to be a problem again. Briggs and his posse hung a couple of them. I don't know where Briggs went after that."

He looked out from under the duster and saw the unsullied expanse of snow. For all he knew, Briggs and his railroad dicks might be scouring the countryside hunting for the robbers they had missed. When they learned of the second robbery, Briggs would be furious. His bosses might even fire him and send another, bigger force out to catch Stringfellow. A rueful smile came to his lips. Stopping Stringfellow no longer stopped the robberies.

"What do you suggest, John? How do I find Stringfellow?" Her jaw tensed as she added, "And Rory. I want to talk to him."

"Are you afraid he'll go into business for himself?"

"Don't be absurd!"

"He knows what it's like firsthand to be a train robber now. And to kill a marshal. He's not making any of it up if he decides to put his exploits down on paper."

"Rory can hardly write his name. Writing an entire novel is beyond him." She got a dark look and glared at Slocum. "There's no way he would be able to find someone else to write his story so he could front for them either."

"You mean he wouldn't be able to cheat on you."

Slocum almost laughed at her expression. He had seen jilted lovers and those who had found their husbands were making time with another woman. Their look was identical to Melissa's. For her writing was more than a job; it was the same as having sex.

"I'll find him, and I'll strangle him with my own hands." She clenched her fingers. They snapped and cracked loud enough to be heard over the fire. Melissa rubbed her hands together, then tucked them under her armpits to keep them warm.

"What's he most inclined to do? Run?"

"No. You said it. He's got the fever now. He'll want to do more than he already has."

"I'd say he has already had a full career of crime, killing a lawman and robbing a train."

"He hasn't robbed a stagecoach," she said. Melissa leaned forward and reached out to take Slocum's arm. "He hasn't robbed a bank."

Slocum pried her hand loose and thought about it.

"We'll head on back to Idaho Falls in the morning, after you've rested up some more."

He had to listen to her cry out in her sleep all night long about how she was going to take her revenge on Rory Randolph. All Slocum could think was that she had no chance for that—if he got to the fake writer first.

"There are three banks in town," Slocum said. "With the marshal dead, we're out of allies. We can't watch all three by ourselves."

"Should you tell the mayor that Marshal Lennox was cut down? He would have a posse formed and they could be on the lookout for Stringfellow and Rory."

"It's better not to scare them off. If you're right that Randolph wants to notch his six-shooter with a bank robbery, a posse roaming around shooting at anything that moves will drive him off. There's no telling where he would go."

"You're right, John. This is our best chance of catching him. Let him think there's nothing standing between him and everything in a bank vault." She muttered "bait" under her breath a few times before subsiding.

Slocum rode down the main street, paying attention to the banks for the first time. Two were side by side, but the third was almost out of town, near the northern edge where businesses were sparse. He rode down the side street toward that bank.

"This one," he said.

"How can you be so sure?"

"It's a cattleman's and rancher's bank, catering to men with a lot of money. We're going into the winter, so whatever they got from selling their herds or crops is likely sitting in a vault waiting for expenses to start up again in the spring."

"How much money do you think is in there?" She licked her chapped lips. A small smile turned downright feral as she considered how a character in her book would knock over the bank. "Do they barge in, guns firing? Or do they break in and dynamite the safe?"

"You know the answer to that," Slocum said.

"Rory wants the thrill of ordering the tellers around and demanding that the president open the safe. He'd never think of blowing it up."

That was the way Slocum saw it, too. When the robbery happened, it would be a bloody one. Just inside the door stood an alert guard with a shotgun cradled in the crook of his arm. Where there was one armed guard, there was likely to be another. This confirmed his guess about how much money had been placed in the bank for safekeeping.

If he warned the banker of a possible robbery, he would be suspected of lying or even plotting to rob the bank himself. Rather than let the president know, warning the guards might be more productive, though they might get trigger happy and shoot anyone who looked like a criminal. On the frontier, that was damned near everyone, including the very ranchers who banked their money here.

"There's an empty store across the street," Slocum said. "We can watch from there."

"I need a gun so I can shoot him down when he goes in."
She ground her teeth together. "No, wait. It's better if I kill
him when he comes out. Then there won't be any question
what he was up to."

"The lives of the tellers and guards are at risk if you let
him rob the bank and come out," Slocum said. "He's gone
plumb loco. Killing them as part of the robbery feeds his
idea of what it's like to be an outlaw."

"I'd kill them all if I were writing the story," she said, nod-
ding. "You have a good sense of plotting, John. What do you
suggest?"

"We watch from the empty store. If Stringfellow is still
leading the gang, he'll want to look over the bank to find its
weaknesses and the best means of getting away."

"There," Melissa said, pointing north. "They'll come
from the north and retreat that way, thinking to lose themselves in the mountains. Getting to Canada will protect them
from any U.S. lawmen."

"They might ride out that way, but they'll circle around and
head south. The storms will make it dangerous to hide in the
hills. One good snowfall and they're trapped. Stringfellow will
convince them they'll have enough money to get through the
winter if they make it south, maybe to Mexico."

"That's a long way off."

Slocum didn't tell her he had considered spending the
winter in the warm sun with even warmer tequila and señoritas. The notion appealed more to him now even if he didn't
have the sort of money Stringfellow and Randolph had riding in their saddlebags. The money from the train robbery
would set him up in style for a long time.

"We can go around back and get into the building that
way. It's not a good idea if any of the bank guards see us.
They'll get suspicious, and we don't want that."

Slocum agreed with her. They rode around to the back
of the store. Slocum stiffened when he saw a horse tethered
there.

"Somebody's got the same idea we do about watching the bank."

"It can't be the marshal. He's dead." Melissa's eyes went wide. "That means it has to be Rory!"

"Or Stringfellow." It didn't matter to him which outlaw was inside. He would find a measure of revenge on either to his liking. "Wait here."

He stepped down and drew his six-shooter before edging to the door. It had been pulled shut but wasn't secured. Using his toe, he pushed it open far enough to take a quick look inside. He couldn't believe his good luck. Rory Randolph crouched down and peered out a spot on the dirty front window he had cleaned off.

Slocum moved like the wind, slipping inside. When he cocked the six-gun, Randolph finally realized he wasn't alone.

"Go for that hogleg and I'll cut you down before you get halfway around. Hands high. Now!" Slocum stepped farther into the dusty room. It had been a yard goods store from the look of the shelves and counters left behind.

"Slocum. You got me fair and square. Are you going to turn me over to the marshal?" Randolph turned and faced him, then laughed. It was an ugly sound. "Wait, you can't. He's dead."

"Lennox was a good man. Did you enjoy shooting him?"

"I loved every second of it," Randolph said. Slocum saw how the crime spree had changed him. He had been big and burly and something of a dandy before. Now only pure mean blazed from his eyes. "I'm gonna love every second of shooting you down, too."

"You've got things mixed up," Slocum said. "I'm the one with the drop on you. When is Stringfellow going to rob the bank?"

"Him and the boys'll be here any time now. He won't let you keep me prisoner."

Slocum wasn't one to make idle threats. If Stringfellow had a ghost of a chance of freeing Randolph, Slocum was willing to shoot the man without an instant's hesitation. If he could kill Stringfellow, too, that would be a bonus.

"So you're nothing more than a lookout. I thought you'd be in the bank, firing your gun and making like a desperado."

"I will be. Wait and see."

Slocum heard the door creak as it opened a bit wider. He took a quick step to the side and glanced at Melissa. He made sure the Colt never left its target dead center on Randolph's chest.

"You betrayed me, Rory. I made you famous. You were living high on the hog, and you turned your back on all that. You . . . you betrayed my *trust*."

"I was your lapdog, Melissa. The money you doled out was like a leash holding me in place. I couldn't steal that much, and I was eating caviar and drinking champagne. But it wasn't because of anything I did. I was only a puppet jumping around when you pulled my strings."

"We need to tie him up," Slocum said. "You can bad-mouth him when he's all hog-tied and not going to do anything we don't want."

"I'll cut his heart out. I'll—"

She never got any further. A bullet smashed the window behind Randolph, sending shards into Slocum's face. He whirled and raised his arm to protect his face. Melissa blundered into him, and they fell to the floor. Slocum pushed her off him and lifted his six-shooter. The room was empty. Randolph had vaulted through the broken window and was running across the street.

"Dammit," Slocum said, getting to his feet.

The bull-throated roar of shotguns discharging sounded in the bank lobby. Then came a returning rifle fire worse than anything he had heard during the war. The bank window exploded out with flying bullets, and cries of fear and pain filled Slocum's ears. He started to follow Randolph through the window, but Melissa grabbed him and pulled him back.

"You'll be shot, John. Don't!"

He saw she was right. Four men stumbled from the bank loaded down with heavy canvas bags. Shotgun fire continued from inside. A guard still worked to stop the robbery. Before one robber could mount, a shotgun blast cut his legs from under him. In return for stopping one, three other outlaws shot the guard.

Slocum saw that one of the men firing so accurately was Will Stringfellow. He steadied his hand, squeezed off a shot, and brought the outlaw leader down.

"You got him. You shot him," Melissa said in a voice almost too low to be heard over the gunfire. "Where's Rory? You have to stop him, too."

Slocum had lost track of Randolph until the man erupted from the front door, dragging a sack of money behind him and firing his six-shooter back into the bank. For an instant he presented a perfect shot for Slocum. His aim was ruined when two of the mounted outlaws spotted Slocum and opened fire on him. Splinters of glass and wood tore at him as the lead sang into the deserted building. Forced to duck, Slocum missed his shot at Randolph.

"No, no, you can't escape. I won't let you!" Melissa boiled out of the store and started to cross the street.

Slocum took it all in with a single glance. Randolph had mounted Stringfellow's horse. The outlaw leader lay dead in the street where Slocum had shot him down. The other robbers fought to keep their horses from rearing. Everything melted together for Slocum. Melissa. Randolph drawing a bead on her. He ran forward, firing wildly in Randolph's direction.

Then he crashed into the woman and knocked her flat. He heard Randolph order the gang to ride out. With Melissa struggling under him, Slocum rose up to get a shot at Randolph. The hammer fell on a spent chamber.

Randolph laughed crazily and fired.

Slocum felt a brief stabbing pain and then the world went away.

18

Slocum winced as pain shot through his head. He forced himself to keep his eyes closed against blinding light and sound so overwhelming it threatened to drive him insane.

"No need to play possum, son. I need the space. Come on, get up."

Slocum winced again at the pain in his side as someone poked him in the rib that had been all shot up. He squinted and turned away from the bright sunlight pouring through a window and saw that he lay on a doctor's table draped in white. Or the cloth had been white once. It was now blood-stained and gray. Turning his face a little more, he saw a wizened old man peering at him through spectacles so thick they magnified his eyes to twice their real size.

The man blinked, poked him again, and said, "You got a rib problem there, son? I missed that. You still got to get your carcass out of here. I've got Miz Larkin on the way in, and she's set to deliver." The man bent closer and whispered, "She's the madam at the town's biggest whorehouse. How she got knocked up is a poser since she's ugly as sin, but then her gals ain't the best lookin' either."

"Whores?"

"Biggest cathouse in Idaho Falls," the man said. "But it's not the best. I prefer the one run by Madam Dubois over on Fleagle Street. Nowhere near the size—it's only a half-dozen cribs—but her gals are a damned sight purtier. And I don't much care she's not really French. Truth is, she's from Detroit and not Paris."

"Who are you?"

"Damn me if that bullet didn't addle your brains," the man said.

Slocum winced again as fingers probed the side of his head, tracing along the line of fire that made his vision blur.

"Just a crease. From what I can see, the wound in your side's just a crease, too. A lucky one, you are, son. Either of those bullets would've kilt you dead if they'd moved over an inch or two. And there's another one almost healed up. Somebody's been usin' you for target practice. Good thing they weren't a better shot. Now get up."

Surprisingly strong hands went under Slocum's arms and pulled him to a sitting position. He wobbled, then the world took shape. He was in a doctor's surgery with anatomical charts hanging on the walls between deer heads and what looked like a stuffed fish.

"That'll be two dollars for my services." The old man held out a bony hand. Slocum fished around until he found the money and handed it over. The hand closed and the money disappeared into a coat pocket. "That there's the way out." The doctor pointed.

Slocum got his feet under him, made sure he had his six-shooter strapped on, and then shuffled to the door. His boot heel was coming loose again. Trying to remember how he had come to be in a doctor's office mattered less to him than getting the boot fixed. He opened the door as two women helped a third—a pregnant woman with a veil over her face—down from a carriage a few feet away. He stepped back, holding the door against the stiff wind. The trio went inside.

One woman flashed him a smile that he would have considered a come-on if he hadn't been so shaky.

He closed the door behind them and let the sharp wind and low temperature wake him fully. He pulled his coat a bit tighter and headed for a saloon. Halfway to the closest one, Melissa Benton called out his name.

Slocum tried to pretend it was only a ghost, something caught on the wind that confused him. When she rushed up, took his arm, and steered him away from the refuge of the gin mill, he had to believe she was real.

"I have a room. You need to rest."

"I did that already. Back there. It cost me two dollars."

"He's the only doctor in town. I feared that he might be a quack, but with you unconscious, I didn't want to take a chance."

"I paid him two dollars." Slocum heard the voice from a distance and only slowly realized he was speaking. Things echoed in his skull, but he was getting his senses back. "I need a drink."

"Yes, yes, but he did a fine job bandaging your poor head." She reached up to touch his wound, but he recoiled. She pulled back her hand and steered him inside the hotel. The warm lobby after the cold outside further shocked him into alertness. "There's a seat by the window. Go and rest. I'll get you a drink."

He sank onto the sofa. From here he had a good view of the main street and the freight wagons moving back and forth. This was a prosperous town, but he knew he couldn't stay. There was nothing for him here. He looked up when Melissa returned. She carried a tray with a pint bottle and drinking glasses on it. With exaggerated care, she put it down on a low table.

"You reacted poorly to loud sounds."

"I'm all right," he said. He waited for her to pour two drinks. He downed one, let the warmth spread throughout his body, and held the glass out for another. The second shot erased most of his aches and pains. "I was afraid I'd die before. Now I think I'll live. That was what I needed."

"Another?"

He wasn't going to deny her the chance to serve him that drink also. After he knocked it back, he leaned against the sofa arm and looked at her. His eyes focused, and she was about the loveliest thing he had ever seen.

"You've taken a bath."

"And changed my clothing. Being on the trail like that was so . . . filthy."

She was a city girl born and bred. She might write about gunslingers and outlaws, but Slocum saw her dancing at some fancy ball or going to the opera and sipping champagne, not cheap rotgut like he was swilling. He took another drink. This one restored him fully.

"Where's Randolph?" He watched a new storm of anger sweep over her.

"He got away. You shot Will Stringfellow, but Rory took his horse and got away with the rest of the robbers."

Slocum chewed on this. Stringfellow was dead, but Randolph had taken his place when it came to men he ought to get even with.

"I can't rightly remember. Was it Randolph that shot me?"

"I don't know. You saved me, John. You protected me. I had my head down as all the lead was flying around. It could have been Rory who shot you. Does it matter?"

"Reckon not," Slocum allowed. "I've reached the point where I'm so shot up, whoever the next one is to put a slug in me hardly matters."

"I don't want you to be shot, John. Really, I don't."

He saw how she edged closer to him, their knees touching. She reached out and lightly laid her hand on his cheek. The touch felt warm. Hot. Her hand moved down his cheek to his chest, then lower until she massaged the growing lump at his crotch.

"You saved my life. I know you did. I want to thank you."

"There's no need."

"I feel your need," she said, squeezing down even more.

Slocum stirred uncomfortably. He tried to sidle away, but she scooted even closer. He smelled the perfume in her hair, the cleanliness of her clothing and body. From this position, he got a good view of the tops of her breasts, now heaving as her excitement mounted with his.

"Come up to my room. We'll be arrested if we keep going here," she said.

"There's no marshal," he pointed out.

She laughed wickedly. "Come up to my room, and I'll lay down the law." In a whisper, she added, "And the law's not all that'll get laid."

A final squeeze on his crotch and she was on her feet and lightly heading up the stairs to the second floor. Slocum watched her bustle sway and how she flashed him a look at her ankle—her calf!—as she paused halfway up the stairs and turned to give him a come-hither look.

He damned himself for a fool, but after all he had been through, he counted lying with Melissa as his due. His reward. The only pay he was ever going to get for being shot and almost dying. He stopped at the bottom of the stairs and looked up at the woman. Melissa had reached the top and began raising her skirts. After giving him a hint of what lay underneath, she turned and faced him. The wicked smile on her lips was enough to make his manhood try to turn cartwheels.

She raised her skirts even more so he saw her knees, her thighs, and higher. She wasn't wearing anything under her skirt.

As slowly as she had revealed her naked readiness for him, she hid it. The skirts fell with a soft sigh. Then she dashed down the hall.

Slocum took the steps two at a time and got to the top in time to see her duck into a room down the hall. He paused when he passed the room where Rory Randolph had been kidnapped. That seemed so long ago. Then his long stride took him to stand in the doorway leading to the woman's room. She had already shucked off her voluminous skirts and stood naked from the waist down.

She looked up, her grin even more wicked than before.

"Help me with my blouse. I want to be completely naked when I rub against you in bed."

Slocum's fingers felt like sausages. Instead of unfastening the delicate pearl buttons one by one, he slid his fingers under the neckline of the blouse and yanked. He ripped the silk and sent the buttons flying about like bullets to bounce off the walls. Melissa closed her eyes, thrust out her chest, and tilted her head back.

"I'm yours, John. Take me. Now!"

He silenced her with a hard kiss. Their lips crushed together and then parted slightly so their tongues could roam back and forth in an erotic dance, going from one mouth to the other and back. His tongue slid over hers and then teased the very tip. He drew back and made a complete circuit of her lips before moving lower. She gasped and melted in his strong arms.

He worked his way into the canyon between her breasts. The flesh flowed as if it were the same silken material of her blouse. But the flesh quivered and came fully alive under his oral assaults. With the area fully kissed and sampled by lips and tongue, he slid lower. With a sudden surge, he swept her off her feet and dropped her on the bed. The woman sank into the feather mattress.

"Oh, oh!"

Her excitement robbed her of words as he worked past her slightly domed belly and pressed on lower. His mouth kissed. His tongue explored. And then he slid between the beckoning pink flaps guarding her inner fastness. The salty, tangy taste spurred him on. He sucked the woman's nether lips between his oral ones and then treated them to constant stimulation using his tongue. She thrashed about and her legs rose up on either side of his head.

And then he was plunged into a delightful world devoid

of sight and sound. Her thighs clamped on his ears, shutting out her passionate moans. With his face buried between her legs, he was robbed of sight. Slocum reveled in the scent and taste and feel of her trembling privates as he drove his tongue in and out of her in imitation of what was to come.

When her legs released him, he looked up. It was as if he spied her lovely face between two white peaks capped with taut nipples.

"Now, John. I can't stand any more of this. I need you inside me."

He reached up and parted her legs. She drew her knees up in wanton invitation. He stood, cast off his gun belt, and pulled down his jeans. He gasped in relief as his erection popped free of the denim prison that his jeans had become. She eyed his crotch and let her tongue make a slow circuit of her red lips to silently urge him on.

Needing no such invitation, he knelt between her bare legs and propped himself up on the bed, one hand on either side of her body. Greedily, she reached between her legs, caught his hard shaft, and insistently tugged it forward. The bulbous tip prodded her. She shuddered at the light touch. Then she screamed out in pure uninhibited desire as he pushed forward. The thick tip parted the lips he had just kissed and then he plunged balls deep into her.

The quick thrust caused a volcanic eruption within her. She clutched so hard at the mattress she tore out sections and sent feathers flying. Slocum hardly noticed. He closed his eyes and let her inner oils soak into his hidden length. She was tight and warm. When she began tensing and relaxing her pussy muscles, he thought she had grabbed him with a hand gloved in velvet.

He pulled back slowly. Every inch was a new and wondrous delight. When only his tip remained within her, he lunged forward again. The intrusion rocked her back on the bed and caused her to lift her legs high in the air, kicking out with her heels. This produced sensations along his entire length that threatened to rob him of control.

With her ankles locked behind his back, she held him firmly in place. Her eyes opened, and tiny trapped-animal noises escaped her lips. She reached up and clawed at his upper arms.

With a quick arching of his back, he entered her fully again. The slow, methodical exit proved harder. She tormented him with her strong inner muscles. Rotating his hips produced a new feeling deep within his balls. It sparked new cries of desire from her. He corkscrewed his way back in, but the withdrawal with no longer slow. He felt the desires running wild in his loins. He began pistoning in and out, moving faster, burning them both up with the loving friction.

Melissa cried out again. She lifted her hips off the bed and rammed them over his impaling, fleshy spike. Slocum began stroking with increased need. He tried to split her apart all the way to the chin. The white heat threatened to consume him from the inside out. When he was sure he could not continue, he found the strength to hold back the flood to get the most pleasure possible from this coupling.

But their movements, their lovemaking savvy, all gave more gratification even as it stole away the chance to continue longer. Slocum grunted as the rush built from the depths of his churning balls and exploded out the tip. She rocked and thrust her hips toward him and finally sank back to the bed.

Slocum sneezed at the feathers flying about. Melissa lifted her hands and sent a double handful flying into the air. She laughed and then put her arms around his neck and pulled him down for a passionate kiss. Slocum rolled to the side, and they lay entwined in a Gordian knot of arms and legs and tongues until even this tuckered them out.

"That was superb, John. I have missed this so much. I don't want to lose out on it any longer."

"What do you mean?"

She came up on an elbow and looked down at him. Her eyes gleamed. She licked her lips before beginning to explain.

"Rory is lost to me. There cannot be any more Rory Randolph novels."

"Write them under your own name."

"I told you the publishers will not take a book from a woman, but they will from a real cowboy named John Slocum."

"You want me to take his place?"

"More. He and I were never . . . never like this. You will be the toast of the town. New York society will clamor for your presence. You will turn down more invitations than you can possibly accept."

"They'll want me at their parties because they'll know what I've done out here?" Slocum wasn't sure that was a good thing. He had wanted posters drifting around with his likeness on them.

"No, silly, they'll want you because you are a writer and know the subject. You'll be the premier Western writer."

"I don't take much to big crowds."

"You'll learn to love the limelight. Rory did, and he was nowhere near as *versatile* as you. You're smart. You'll fit right in after a season. And a few books, of course, but that won't be a problem. I've almost written another one while traipsing about in these horrid mountains. Why, a book about being captive of savages will be an immediate bestseller."

"Captive?"

"You sold me to the Indian chief. The story from that will scandalize the publisher. It will become an instant classic of its kind."

"You're going to pay me, too? For doing nothing but showing up at these parties? I wouldn't be writing the books."

"Of course you wouldn't be writing. No offense, but your

education is hardly the equal of a single quickly penned novel, no matter how much a potboiler it is." She sat up in bed. He was fascinated with the way her breasts swayed as she gestured. "You won't want for money. I make a fine living."

"So you'd be keeping me?"

"In the greatest of luxury." She turned and bent low, her lips kissing his belly. Her hot breath stirred his manhood, but it was too soon yet to rise once more. "You'd be in luxury and share my bed. Rory never did that. He was simply too uncouth, and truth to tell, despite his violent background, I found him far too pliant. Not a coward, but almost that."

She ran her fingers around through the hair on his belly, then gripped his crotch and began rhythmically squeezing life into it again.

"No one can ever claim you are a coward, John. Never."

"Glad to hear that."

"And I'm glad to hear that you agree to come with me. The stage is leaving the first thing tomorrow morning for the docks on the Missouri. We can catch a riverboat there before the storms get too bad. The stagecoach agent said a new storm might isolate Idaho Falls for days, and we'd miss the chance to return to the East, possibly until next spring. I won't spend the winter in this hellhole."

"I agree," he said. Idaho Falls was too big for his liking. There might be a thousand people calling this home.

"Wonderful," she said, clapping her hands. "I need to pack for tomorrow's departure."

"I have to tend my horse," he said.

"Oh, yes, sell that smelly beast. You might make a few dollars from it. But whatever you do, come back tonight. We can sleep in until almost time for the stagecoach to leave. Then it's going to be a marvelous journey all the way home. You cannot believe what it's like to make love in a Pullman car. Or in the presidential suite aboard a riverboat."

Slocum got out of bed, pulled up his pants, and buttoned

the fly. He settled the gun belt around his middle, then went to the window when he heard the thunder of hooves out in the street.

"It's Sonny Briggs and his posse," he said.

"I should go find out what they have been up to," she said, lounging back, naked. Wisps of her torn blouse hung on her shoulders. Already the cold in the room caused gooseflesh to pop up on her bare breasts and turn the copper-colored nipples taut.

"I'll see what they've found."

She stared at him, her face hardening.

"Do that, John. Go on a bender with them if you like. Just be here tomorrow morning."

"Tomorrow," he said.

Slocum stepped out into the corridor, hesitated as he stared at the closed door, and softly said, "Tomorrow."

Then he went downstairs to talk with Briggs.

19

Slocum stepped out into the wind and shivered. He had gone from a hot room upstairs to being surrounded by ice. No sooner had he left the hotel than Briggs saw him and motioned for him to go over. Slocum turned up the collar on his coat, wishing he had on his duster, too.

"We just rode in, Slocum, and heard the bank got robbed."

"Good to see you, too, Briggs," Slocum said. He grabbed his hat to keep it from flying away. The railroad detective saw the bandage on his head and touched his own in question. "Got shot up at the bank robbery."

"Heard that Stringfellow got shot. That your doin'?"

Slocum nodded.

"I talked to the bank president, and he said the writer fellow lit out at the head of the gang. Has he taken over?"

"He's on a tear," Slocum said. "Ever since he shot down the marshal." He saw the shock on Briggs's face at this.

"I've been on the gang's trail and hadn't heard. You bury Lennox out in the hills?"

"If he's got a next of kin, it'd be good if you let them know."

"I haven't been in town as long as you." Sonny Briggs barked at his men and sent them off on errands, then dismounted. "You evened the score with Stringfellow. You intending on tracking down the writer?"

Slocum looked up at the hotel window, almost expecting to see Melissa there watching. The curtains moved as wind whistled past the window frame, but other than that, there wasn't any hint the room had seen any occupants today or ever.

"I've been giving it some consideration."

"Me and the boys are headin' straight out again. You have any ideas about where Randolph might run?"

"He's got a fair amount of money, but that's not what's driving him," Slocum said.

"The main office wired back that the train was held up and a powerful lot of money was stolen. The engineer said you and the marshal shot it out with the robbers but couldn't stop them. You're a good man, Slocum. You want to ride with us? I can see that the railroad hires you on at top dollar."

"We tracked Stringfellow and Randolph and that's when the marshal was killed," Slocum said. He pressed his hand into his side. He had taken more than his share of lead.

"Fifty dollars a month to help us bring Randolph to trial."

"And is there a reward for getting the haul from the train back?"

"I'll see that you get a hundred dollars."

From the way Briggs said it, the reward was bigger, but Slocum wasn't going to dicker. He looked back up at the hotel room.

"I can get you on the trail, but I've got somewhere to be tomorrow morning."

"You do that and I'd be much obliged."

Briggs got his men circled around and made sure they had enough supplies for at least a week on the trail. After he got him men mounted, Briggs look questioningly at Slocum.

"I'll fetch my horse. It's staked out behind the building across the street from the bank."

Briggs and his posse trotted ahead. Slocum cut through an alley and reached the spot where both his and Melissa's horses were tethered. He had been afraid someone would steal the animals. He mounted, then caught up the reins to Melissa's horse, and tugged to get it following. She wasn't going to need it, and on the trail a spare horse let him ride along until one tired, then switch off. This would serve him in good stead getting back to town. He could cover twice the distance and join Melissa on the stage going south the next day.

He rounded the building. Briggs whipped his men up into getting back on the trail of the robbers in spite of having been in the hills for so long.

"You catch any of Stringfellow's gang?" Slocum asked as he rode alongside Briggs on their way out of town.

"Didn't even catch sight after we run down a pair of them. We thought we had all of them after the first robbery attempt. We should have gone along on the train rather than the wild-goose chase."

"They know these mountains better 'n anyone I know," Slocum said. He pointed to the ground. "They weren't trying to cover their tracks."

"It gets rocky not too far."

Slocum rode along, thinking hard about his future. He didn't feel easy with the posse, tracking outlaws alongside Sonny Briggs. The reward the railroad man offered was as much as he had earned all summer long working as a wrangler. With Rory Randolph leading the gang, finding him would be easy. He lacked Will Stringfellow's frontier skills, and the others in the gang were followers, not thinkers.

If he turned around, he could get back to Idaho Falls before midnight and spend the night with Melissa. To leave with her to New York to become an acclaimed writer. Acclaimed for something he didn't do. But he would be rich, and sharing a bed with such a lovely woman had its appeal.

"There," Slocum said, pointing up into the hills. "They camped ten miles off in that direction before. Randolph's not smart enough to find a new campsite. If you ride carefully, you can reach them by dawn."

"Come with us, Slocum. Think of the money. And you can avenge Lennox's death. That's got to be eating away at you."

Slocum found no tears to shed for the dead marshal. The man had died doing his job. Given time, the two of them might have become fast friends. On the trail they had watched each other's backs. Partners, without being partners in the truest sense. But risking his own life to avenge Lennox?

That wasn't in him.

"Your men can handle the gang. As much as I'd like to get Randolph in my sights, knowing you got him is good enough."

"You have somewhere you have to be?"

Slocum looked from Briggs back over his shoulder in the direction of Idaho Falls.

"Reckon so. I want to get there by sunup." Slocum rode closer and thrust out his hand. He and Briggs shook. "Good luck with them. All of them."

"For you, Slocum, and for the marshal. We'll get them all."

Slocum watched the posse start up a slope in the direction of the old camp Stringfellow had used, then he tugged on his pinto's reins, turned, and started on a different trail.

An hour after dawn, he drew rein and waited for the riders to meet him.

"Howdy," Slocum said. "I wondered if there was room for one more to winter with your tribe."

Lost Horse looked from Slocum to Melissa's horse, then shrugged.

Slocum handed over the reins.

"A gift for my brother."

"Welcome, brother," the Cree brave said, grinning. "You are in time to join the hunting party."

This suited Slocum just fine. He wasn't cut out to be a lawman and he certainly wasn't cut out to be a kept man pretending to be something he wasn't. All the French champagne in the world—and even Melissa to drink it with him—wasn't enough.

"Have you found the meadow to the north where there are more deer than you can eat all winter long?"

Lost Horse made a disparaging remark about optimistic white men, and Slocum laughed. This was where he belonged, at least until spring. Then he could decide where to ride. He had no idea where that might be, but it wasn't going to be New York.

Watch for

SLOCUM AND THE BIG TIMBER TERROR

428th novel in the exciting SLOCUM series
from Jove

Coming in October!

GIANT-SIZED ADVENTURE FROM AVENGING ANGEL LONGARM.

BY TABOR EVANS

penguin.com/actionwesterns